Tor books by Christopher Pike

*Sati*
*The Season of Passage*\*

\*forthcoming

# CHRISTOPHER PIKE

## SATI

A TOM DOHERTY ASSOCIATES BOOK
NEW YORK

# Sati is pronounced SAH-tee.

SATI

Copyright © 1990 by Christopher Pike.

A Tor Book
Published by Tom Doherty Associates, Inc.
49 West 24th Street
New York, N.Y. 10010

Cover art by Scott Hague

ISBN: 0-812-51035-6
Library of Congress Catalog Card Number: 90-42332

First edition: October 1990
First mass market printing: July 1991

Printed in the United States of America

0  9  8  7  6  5  4  3  2  1

*For Maharishi*

# SATI

# Chapter 1

I once knew this girl who thought she was God. She didn't give sight to the blind or raise the dead. She didn't even teach anything, not really, and she never told me anything I probably didn't already know. On the other hand, she didn't expect to be worshiped, nor did she ask for money. Given her high opinion of herself, some might call that a miracle. I don't know, maybe she was God. Her name was Sati and she had blond hair and blue eyes.

I first met her in the middle of the night alongside Highway 10 in the Arizona desert. She was sitting—not standing like your usual hitchhiker—in the sand next to the asphalt. Had I been any more tired than I already was, I probably would have missed her. All I saw was a flash of white in my semi's high beams. I was a couple of seconds down the road before I realized I'd just passed a person. My brakes took their time bringing my seventy-mile-per-hour rig to a halt. In the rearview mirror, my flash of white stood and walked slowly toward the truck.

When the passenger door opened a minute later, and the overhead light went on, I decided I'd made a wise decision stopping.

She was a soft beauty, and I blinked twice, for she looked familiar, though later, I was never able to decide who she reminded me of. The rose tinge of her skin complemented her long sunny hair. Her big eyes glanced across my littered seat, bright and calm.

"Need a ride?" I asked.

She nodded, lifting up the hem of her white dress and sliding into the seat. The overhead light went off as she shut the door.

"Are you hitchhiking?" I asked, thinking I hadn't seen any broken-down car along the road.

"Yes," she said.

"Well, I'm heading to L.A."

"I have friends in L.A."

"You want to ride all the way there with me?"

"Yes," she said.

That was fine with me. Hauling freight when you're half asleep is always easier with company. I put the truck into gear and we rolled forward.

# SATI

"My name's Michael Winters," I said, offering my hand, hoping she could see it in the dark. Desert nights get as deep as a pool of ink. Her profile was a shadow against the black window. Her warm fingers found mine and squeezed hello.

"I'm Sati," she said.

"Oh." I say *oh* a lot. The world is always taking me by surprise. "What kind of name is Sati?"

"An old one."

"How did you come to be sitting out here at this time of night?"

"I was waiting for a ride."

Her tone was not unhappy, but she was obviously being evasive. Perhaps she'd just had a fight with her boyfriend and had been dumped, I thought. Or maybe she lived in Catson, a town a few miles back the way I'd come, and had decided to leave home tonight. She couldn't have been more than twenty.

"Hey, you hungry?" I asked. There was a diner not far up ahead where I occasionally stopped during my boring Phoenix to L.A. runs. Before picking up my guest, I hadn't planned on eating so soon. I think I just wanted to get another good look at her.

"I wouldn't mind stopping," Sati said.

Pete's was the name of the place, appropriately enough; it served tons of truck drivers who resembled the owner and head chef Peter Korboff, a big heavyset man whose sole culinary achievement was consistently fantastic

3

pancakes. I usually stopped in only when I knew the diner would be fairly empty. Just because I made my living moving freight from one town to another didn't mean I was a truck driver. The job was temporary, I told myself. And the years kept rolling by.

The air had a chill in it as we climbed out. Come ten in the morning and I knew it would be simmering. Sati pulled up beside me, a head shorter than my even six feet. Her long white dress swished close to the pavement as we walked toward the diner's front door.

"I hope Penny's working," I said.

Sati nodded, apparently not caring who Penny was.

The place was crowded for two in the morning. There were about a dozen people present. Steering Sati toward a booth in the corner, I noticed Penny pouring coffee behind the counter and gave a wave. She raised an eyebrow when she saw I had a female with me. Penny was a good friend—we'd spoken to each other once a week for the last three years—but she didn't know my wife was divorcing me. I hate telling people my problems. It depresses me.

"I see you don't have a purse," I told Sati when we were seated. The hard white light of the diner took nothing away from her beauty. Her complexion looked as soft as it had during my first glimpse of her in the truck. At my remark, her wide mouth curled into an amused line. I added hastily, "But don't worry if you're hungry. I've got money."

"I'm not worried, Michael," she said.

"All right."

Sati wasn't a large girl, but her fingers were long and slim. The way she tugged at her bright hair while gazing distractedly about struck me as charming in a little-girl sort of way. She wasn't wearing a ring.

Penny brought us menus and water a moment later. Penny was destined to be a waitress in a truck stop coffee shop. She fit the part so well. Buxom, with cheaply dyed red hair and gobs of makeup, she had the friendly southern accent that barely hid a lonely pain. Her husband had died of cancer a week after their fifth anniversary, and she had never remarried. Her twenty-year-old son was presently doing time in a sweaty Texas jail for stealing a car. Had Harry Chapin still been alive, he might have written a song about her.

"And who do we have here, Mike?" Penny asked.

"A lost hitchhiker who thinks she wants to go to L.A.," I said. "Penny, meet Sati."

"Lord, girl, don't tell me you're another one of those aspiring actresses?" Penny said. "I see dozens of them pass through here on their way to fame and fortune. See them on their way home, too, the stars washed from their eyes. Where're you from, child?"

"Not far from here," Sati said.

Penny gave her a closer look, puzzled. "Have I seen you before?"

Sati did not answer the question. She instead nodded to the ring on Penny's finger, a plain gold band given to Penny on her wedding day. "The ring is very nice," Sati said.

Penny fairly lit up, then laughed. "I can see you know nothing about jewelry, girl. Try to hock this in L.A. and you would hardly have enough to buy yourself lunch."

Sati stared her straight in the eye. It was then I realized what had struck me about her blue eyes the moment she had climbed in my truck. They were unusually serene. I wondered if she was stoned.

"But you wear it well," Sati said.

Penny seemed touched. "Thank you," she said softly. Then, shaking herself as if she was stirring from a pleasant daydream, she reached for her pad. "So, Mike, what would you and your traveling companion like this fine morning?"

"I'll have six of Pete's perfect pancakes and a cup of coffee," I said. "Bring lots of butter."

"I should have known. Sati?"

Sati had been looking out the window. She glanced toward the counter. "May I have that banana, there?"

"Is that all you want?" I asked.

"Better take a free meal when you can get one," Penny said. Sati nodded, as though that were good advice, but didn't say anything. Penny added, "Are you a vegetarian? I know a

6

lot of actresses are. Listen, I could put that banana on some cold cereal if you'd like?"

"That would be fine," Sati said.

Penny collected our menus and left. "You're not really an actress, are you?" I asked.

"Not exactly," Sati said.

"What do you plan on doing in L.A.?"

"I'll tell you when we get there."

"You don't know?"

She smiled again. Like her tugging at her hair, it seemed so innocent, that smile. For a moment I thought she could have been an actress, that she could have lit up any screen. "I know," she said.

Our food came and I ate quickly. Penny had diced the banana over a bowl of cornflakes and drenched it in milk. Sati chewed each bite so thoroughly one would have thought she believed it was going to be her last meal for the rest of the week. My plate was clean and I was finishing my second cup of coffee, feeling anxious to hit the road, when she finally pushed her bowl away.

"We can go," she said.

"You're full?" Her bowl wasn't empty.

"Completely full."

Just before we stood to leave, I noticed a pot bellied man with a handlebar moustache standing by the door and staring our way. It took me a moment, but then I recognized him as a local, a foreman in a factory in Catson who always worked the late shift. We'd shared a cup of coffee at the counter before, although I couldn't remember what his name was. He appeared on the verge of approaching us, but he suddenly turned and left.

"Did you see that guy?" I asked.

"Which guy was that?" Sati asked innocently.

"Never mind, he's gone."

Penny returned to our table to say goodbye. She told me to give Linda her love. I left a tip as big as the bill. I like to tip big; it makes me feel like a nice guy.

Sati and I were back in the truck and barreling down the road when Sati asked about Linda.

"She's my wife," I said. "We've known each other since high school. We have a daughter named Jenny. She'll be six next month, June seventeenth. We had her only a year after we were married."

Actually, we'd had Jenny only nine months after we'd been married, but tell people that and they think they know what really happened. Back then, Linda and I both had to drop out of college and get jobs. I'd never had a chance to get back and Linda was only now finishing her degree. One of her professors was her new boyfriend. She had always fancied the academic types. His name was Dick.

"You would like Jenny," I added. "She's the smartest little kid."

"What about Linda?" Sati asked.

Sati's question caught me off guard. I wasn't exactly sure what she was asking. Nevertheless, the query did give me an occasion to examine my motives in picking her up. There was the company excuse, sure, but I'd never bought a hitchhiker breakfast before. What the hell, I thought, her long dress wasn't giving away a lot, but there was no hiding her fine figure.

I'd slept with two women in the six months since I had split up with Linda. I'd thought there was a chance my depression was largely sexual frustration. I'd thought wrong, and had not called Sharon or Joetta back. Glancing across the dark seat, I wondered if I was ever going to learn. Sati's hair hung loosely atop her breasts.

"What?" I said.

"Linda must be smart, too."

I decided she was playing with me. "Tell me about yourself."

Sati wore what appeared to be hand-carved wooden slippers. Slipping her feet out of them, she tucked her legs beneath her and sat cross-legged on the seat. "I'll tell you when we get to your apartment," she said.

"But I'm not going straight to my apartment. We've got several tons of pool acid sitting a few feet behind us. I've got to drop that off first."

"Fine."

"But afterward, if you'd like, I could take you over to your friends'."

She closed her eyes and sat up straight. "I'm going to your apartment. Don't talk to me until we get there."

"But what about your friends?" I asked.

"You are my friend, Michael."

9

* * *

The sun had begun to color the sky when I backed into Stenson's Pool Supply dock. Mr. Stenson was one of my more dependable customers. Twice a week he had me bringing in a full trailer of goods from Phoenix. He intended to give me more business when I purchased two more trucks, which would give me four altogether. At present, my partner, Jesse, drove my other truck. Stenson was a reference I planned on using when I hit the bank later on in the day with my hand out begging for money. Here I hated what I was doing, and I was trying to expand the business. Don't ask me why.

Sati had a strong back. Her posture stayed firm the whole time she slept. I wondered if she wasn't really meditating or something. She didn't move an inch, I swear.

I couldn't have counted the times I glanced over at her.

Stenson's son was already at work. With his help, I had the acid unloaded in fifteen minutes. He didn't have occasion to look up front. He had no idea I had a cute blond with me. Not that I would have cared. My fatigue level had begun to reach the point where sleep, more than any imaginable erotic encounter, was all I wanted. I'd already decided Sati could crash at my place for a day or two. She didn't seem the sort who was going to steal me blind. Of course, my wife hadn't seemed that sort either, until her boyfriend had introduced her to his lawyer.

"Sati," I said softly as we approached my

home. My apartment's in a small complex in Santa Monica, about half a mile from the beach. The place was owned by a high school buddy of mine, David Stone. My friendship with David was the main reason I was living there, although he didn't give me a break on the rent. David had a lot of money, and kept an eye on it.

Sati opened her eyes at the sound of her name. She stared off into space for a moment, then closed them again. "We're almost there," she whispered.

"Yeah. Did you have a nice rest?"

She opened her eyes again and glanced out her window. The eastern sky was orange going on yellow. "Yes. It's going to be a pretty day, a busy day."

"Do you have plans?"

She regarded me thoughtfully, without a trace of drowsiness in her eyes. "Yes."

"What are you going to do?" I asked.

"You'll see, after you sleep."

My trailers are far too big to park at the apartment complex where I live. I was currently renting a square of asphalt that belonged to a nearby car dealer. The parking spot was ideal. It was only a short walk to my place. I didn't have to go through the hassle of unhooking the trailers from the truck every time I came home.

As I had surmised, Sati's slippers were definitely wooden. They made funny knocking sounds after we'd parked and were walking along the sidewalk. "Where did you get those shoes?" I asked.

"I made them."

"Really?"

"I made this dress, too," she said.

"You must be pretty handy."

"Oh, I am."

Fred McDougal was in front of the apartments folding papers. He worked for the *Times*, and also helped David Stone maintain the grounds, for which David let him have a tiny apartment for free. Fred was nineteen, but still finishing his senior year in high school. His dad had thrown him out of the house a few months back and he had latched onto me as sort of an authority figure. That was fine with me. Fred was a nice kid. He had girl troubles, too. Lori was her name, and I doubt she had any idea how much I knew about her. The problem was, Lori didn't feel the same way Fred did. It was a common problem.

"You should be on your way by now," I told Fred, checking my watch. It was half past five. Fred was usually done folding his papers by five. He'd already almost lost his job the previous month for chucking a five-pound Sunday edition at a thousand-dollar miniature poodle. He'd broken the dog's collar bone.

"My station wagon's busted," he said, brushing aside his long sweaty brown hair. Fred and I looked somewhat alike, and many of the things he said reminded me of myself at an early age—say, when I was fourteen or so. Fred wasn't especially bright. Our coloring and height were alike, and we were both slender, with broad shoulders. But Fred had a terrible slouch, and he wasn't nearly as handsome as I am. I'm not being vain. I'm truly sorry to say Lori would have agreed with my assessment. Fred's pimples were all over the place. He ate too much junk food.

"Did you tell Nick?" I asked. Nick Chevas was another high school chum of mine. He lived downstairs from me.

"Mary says he won't be back until this afternoon," Fred said. Mary Dorado was Nick's live-in girlfriend.

"I don't know what we're going to do," I said. "My car's in the shop. And you're already late. How come you're only folding the papers now?"

"I've been busy trying to find a car," Fred said, worried, glancing at Sati for the first time.

"Did you call your boss?" I asked. "Maybe he could help you out."

Fred shook his head. "He's pissed at me. He's making me pay for that poodle's shoulder brace out of my paycheck. He'd just as soon fire me. What am I going to do?"

Sati spoke up. "Let's use your big truck, Michael."

The thought had occurred to me. Had I been less tired, I probably would have suggested it already, though it wouldn't be much fun on the gears weaving in and out of the neighborhood's narrow streets.

"I can't drive it," Fred said.

"I'll take you," I said, yawning. I turned in the direction of my parked trucks. "Let me unhook the trailers. I'll be back in a few minutes."

Sati stopped me, touching my arm. "I'll take him," she said. "You sleep."

I chuckled. "And I suppose you can handle my tractor?"

"Yes."

Her confident tone took me back a step. "Where's your Class One license? Do you have it in your pocket?"

Sati smiled. "I don't have any pockets." She glanced at Fred. "I'm Sati."

"I'm Fred."

She stuck out her hand in my direction. "May I have the keys, please?"

"But the trailers need disconnecting," I said. "Or do you know how to do that, also?"

"I do," she said.

I don't know why I gave her the keys. Perhaps I wanted to see her face when she came back without the tractor. Fred and I watched as she disappeared around the corner.

"God, where did you find her?" Fred asked. "She's beautiful."

Naturally, living thirty yards away, Fred was aware of my difficulty with Linda. Yet he was under the impression the separation was temporary. "In the middle of nowhere," I said.

"Nice of her to want to help me."

"Yeah, it is," I muttered. "I sure wouldn't mind hitting the sack this minute."

"Were you up all night?"

"Yeah."

"That's rough. So was I. Lori and I got in a big fight last night."

I knew without asking what the fight was about, and that Lori hadn't lost any sleep over it. "They say things get worse before they get better," I said sympathetically.

Fred shook his head. "She went out with another guy last Friday. I don't know why she waited until yesterday to tell me."

Yesterday would have been Sunday. "I don't know why she had to tell you at all," I said.

Fred was disappointed in me. "Don't you think honesty is everything in a relationship?"

I sat down on the curb, resting my weary head in my hands, and thought of all the times my wife had told me exactly what was on her mind. "No," I said.

Sati was back ten minutes later, driving the tractor with practiced ease. She parked right in front of us. She had unhooked the trailers quicker than I could have. "How come you're not in bed?" she called out the window.

I stood, a fresh believer. "I'm going. As long as you're sure you know what you're doing?"

"Sleep, Michael," she said. "Dream pretty pictures."

I nodded, yawning. "Whatever you say. Sati, when you're done, Fred will show you where I live. I'll leave the front door unlocked." I patted Fred on the shoulder. "Better get going."

Fred nodded. "So, what do you think I should do about Lori?"

"Ask Sati. She's a girl."

My apartment has two bedrooms. One was completely crammed with the furniture and appliances that I had inherited during my separation from Linda. Once inside, I wondered if I should leave the usable bedroom to Sati and crash on the couch. It was a fleeting thought. One could push the hospitality routine a bit too far, I decided. Really, when I thought about it, I couldn't figure out why I had instinctively trusted her so quickly.

As I fell asleep, the only pretty picture I remembered thinking of was of her face.

# Chapter 2

And then Linda was sitting beside me and smiling the way she used to smile before the dark ages. Her hair was as black as deep space and an artist had stolen the color of her lips from a red rose. Or so I fancied as I slowly climbed back to waking. "What?" I croaked.

"You were snoring," Linda said.

"Impossible. I never snore." It was nice seeing her before I had to see anything else.

"Hah. I remember different."

"I remember . . ." I muttered, not knowing where to go with it.

"Don't you know you have Jenny this afternoon?" she asked, sitting back and taking her hand off my arm.

"What time is it?"

"Ten. When did you get in?"

I sat up. "Feels like a minute ago."

"You shouldn't be working so much."

"It's hard keeping two roofs over our heads," I said.

That was a mistake, silly me. Linda's voice changed, and not for the better. "If you want to go back to sleep, fine with me. I can take Jenny with me."

There was a note of finality in the remark. "Where is she?"

"Downstairs, cutting flowers with Mrs. Hutchinson."

Mrs. Hutchinson was an elderly widow whom David Stone had made his apartment manager. Except for her always trying to save my soul, we got along OK. But she had never cared much for Linda.

"I'll take her," I said.

"Are you sure? Dick said she could come with us if you were busy."

There was a lousy taste in my mouth. "I'm sure. Where are you two going?"

"Shopping," Linda said.

"Oh, yeah, my birthday's coming up."

Linda winced. "I'm sorry, Mike. When was it? Saturday? It just slipped my mind."

I wondered why Linda hadn't run into Sati out on the couch, and if my truck was still in one piece. "You can get me something extra special for Christmas," I said, climbing out of

18

the bed, missing only my shoes to be fully dressed.

Linda followed me into the kitchen, where I poured myself a glass of orange juice and gargled with it. She sat at the table and studied me. She was fond of studying people. She wanted to be a psychologist. All her schooling had given her the profound insight that I was upset about her leaving.

"You're mad at me," she said.

I spat out the juice. "I'm tired."

Linda sighed. "Let's not fight."

"I'm too tired to fight."

"I said I'd take Jenny."

"Jenny doesn't make me tired," I said.

"Well, obviously I do. You should be happy I moved out."

"I thought I moved out."

Linda groaned impatiently. "Let's not get started. You remember Jenny has an appointment at two with Dr. McAllister?"

McAllister was a child psychologist. He was studying my daughter. She was having nightmares. He had decided it was because of the breakup. He charged sixty dollars for thirty minutes.

"I'll take her if she wants to go," I said.

Linda was firm. "She's going. You don't have to listen to her when she wakes up in the night crying."

"You're right. When she stays here, she never wakes up in the night."

"Dick says . . ."

"Screw Dick."

Linda stood. "I'm going."

"All right. But leave Jenny."

Linda glared at me. She could look awfully sexy when she was mad. There was a time when I used to try to get her angry just so I could look at her. It used to take a lot of work. Now I barely had to try. Some things get easier with age, I suppose.

"I don't think so," she said.

"Leave her here and buy me a birthday card when you're out. You can mail it to me. I can blame the delay on the post office."

Linda headed for the door. I drank the remainder of my orange juice and went after her. Linda was fast on her feet. I only caught up with her when she was downstairs beside Mrs. Hutchinson's rose bushes. Under the careful direction of Mrs. Hutchinson, Jenny was sitting on the ground and scraping the thorns off the stems with a butter knife. A half-filled vase of thornless flowers rested beside her on the grass. Jenny had inherited her mother's features: round cheeks, a button nose, full lips. I'd always been thankful for that—she was darling. Her thick dark hair reached to her waist. I'd told Linda once if she ever cut it there would be no more alimony.

Seeing me, Jenny jumped up and gave me a hug. Behind us, Linda simmered, knowing that I was going to get my way. At least for today.

"Daddy, why aren't you sleeping?" Jenny asked.

"Because that wicked man your mother's seeing says there is to be no rest for your poor daddy until . . ."

"Mike!" Linda said.

"I'm not tired," I told my daughter, squeezing her tightly. And for a moment, I really wasn't. I felt just fine.

"I heard you coming in this morning," Mrs. Hutchinson said, scissors in her wrinkled hand, a note of approval in her voice. She was a firm believer in hard work. She was seventy-three, and up until two years earlier, she had worked full-time as a tailor in an expensive clothes store in Beverly Hills. Arthritic fingers had finally made her throw in the sewing needles. The scissors she was holding were for Jenny's use. She no longer had the strength to squeeze them shut.

I let go of Jenny. "And I smelled your coffee on my way up the stairs," I said. "It made me want to stop in and say hello." I nodded to her rose bushes. "I love those flowers. I don't know anyone who can bring them to life like you." I'm such a smooth dude. It was no wonder the old lady liked me, even with my cursed and unbelieving soul.

Mrs. Hutchinson beamed. "Thank you. I've told your daughter she was to set aside a special dozen for you."

"See, daddy, where one of them bit me," Jenny said, showing me her blood-smeared thumb. I gave it a kiss, wondering again where Sati was.

21

"That's very kind of you," I said to Mrs. Hutchinson. "By the way, have you seen Fred since he finished his paper route?"

"A moment ago. He was returning from the supermarket."

"A moment ago? He mustn't have gone to school."

"That he certainly did not do," Mrs. Hutchinson said, not pleased. "He had some girl with him."

"A blond?"

"That's the one."

I glanced at Linda, who was not enjoying being ignored. "Could you wait here a sec?" I asked. "I have to check on something."

"Do you know this girl?" Linda asked. She'd always had uncanny radar.

"Not really. But just give me a minute."

In the closet-like apartment that David Stone had given to Fred in exchange for neatly trimmed lawns and a carefully maintained swimming pool, I found Sati rolling dough and Fred opening a jar of cherries. Fred jumped a little when I entered. The door had been left open and I hadn't knocked. Sati paused long enough to wave hello with her rolling pin.

"Get the papers delivered?" I asked.

"Yeah," Fred said quickly.

"Good," I said. "How's the truck?"

"I put it back in your parking spot," Sati said. "The keys are on top of your icebox."

"Any problems?" I asked.

"No," she said.

"Great." I sat down. Something was going on. Fred wouldn't look at me. "What happened to school?"

"I didn't go," Fred said.

"Right. Why didn't you go?"

Fred glanced at Sati. She had put her hair up in a bun. Her white dress was sprinkled with white flour.

"He's helping me get ready for tonight," she said.

"Tonight?" I said. "What's tonight?"

"We're having refreshments tonight after my meeting," she said.

"What meeting?" I asked.

Now Fred was looking at the floor. Sati, however, was as cool as ever. "Fred," she said, "give Michael one of our flyers."

"I don't know," Fred said.

Sati smiled at his discomfort. "I'll give him one," she said. Wiping her hands on a dish towel, she removed a notebook-sized sheet from the top of Fred's waist-high icebox and took a seat beside me. She handed me the paper. The lettering was standard typewriter characters. The page was obviously a photocopy.

### ATTENTION!

My name is Sati. I am God. I would like to invite you to a special meeting I will be holding tonight at eight o'clock at 1245 3rd Street, apartment 3. Refreshments will be served.

I am looking forward to meeting with as many of you as possible.

I stared at Sati for a moment.

"I thought you said you weren't an actress?" I said.

"I'm not," she said.

"*This* is apartment three. You couldn't fit five people in here."

"Then we'll have the meeting at your place," she said.

I folded the flyer in two and frowned. "What are you up to?"

Her big blue eyes were mischievous. "Come to the meeting and find out."

I snorted. "Who will be there? Who's seen these flyers besides us?"

"Many of the people on Fred's paper route," she said.

"What?" I exclaimed. "Fred, you didn't put them in with your papers?"

Fred was talking to the wall. "We didn't exactly put them inside the papers."

"We put them on the outside," Sati explained. "Underneath the rubber band. I think the flyer is catchy. I typed it on Fred's typewriter right after you went to bed. I made copies at the Seven-Eleven store around the corner."

Had the circumstances been different, I probably wouldn't have blown up. If someone thinks she's God and wants to tell others, that's her business. But Linda's waking me up and talking about Dick a minute later had put me in a bad mood. Plus I wasn't exactly full of physical pep. In fact, I suddenly had a splitting headache.

"Sati, do you have any idea what you've done?" I asked, not even trying to disguise my anger.

"I know," she said.

"Quit telling me that! You know nothing! Just last week this young man here flattened a poodle. He came within an inch of getting fired. And that was an accident. How do you think the *Times* is going to feel about having this garbage purposely peddled inside their paper?"

"No one will complain to the paper," Sati said, unmoved by my outburst.

"You don't know that!"

"But I do."

"Don't get mad, Mike," Fred said meekly. "I've never had a party here before. I'd kind of like one."

"She's not talking about a party! She's talking about a goddamn meeting!"

Sati smiled. "It won't be a goddamn meeting. It's a meeting about myself."

"But you say you're God!" I said.

In soap operas, people always walk in on arguments at precisely the worst moment. The same axiom applies to my life. In the blink of an eye, Linda, Jenny, and Mrs. Hutchinson were standing in the doorway. "Who says they're God?" Mrs. Hutchinson wanted to know.

Sati plucked the flyer from my paws and handed it to the old lady, casually returning to her rolling pin and cookie dough. Linda crowded beside Mrs. Hutchinson. Together the two of them read the good news for modern man, their faces quickly darkening. Jenny stood staring at Sati in awe, a bunch of red roses in her tiny hands.

"Did you write this?" Mrs. Hutchinson demanded, her eyes narrowing on Sati.

"Yes." Sati sprinkled a little sugar over her dough. "You are also welcome to attend the meeting."

"This is blasphemy," Mrs. Hutchinson breathed, trembling. Because she was so old, I worried about her heart, which made me all the angrier at Sati.

"This is ridiculous," Linda snickered. "Mike, who is this girl?"

My attention was drawn to my daughter. Her awed expression was frozen on her face. She stood mesmerized, watching Sati make her cookies. "I don't know," I said to Linda.

"He picked up Sati last night on his way home," Fred said with his usual good timing.

"Is that true?" Linda asked.

"Yes," Sati said, with no skin off her back.

"Swell," Linda said. "You're to watch your daughter for the day and you bring home a blond to play with."

I got to my feet and yelled at my wife. "She's not a blond I brought home to play with! She's just a girl. She needed a ride. I was trying to help her out, all right? What's wrong with that?"

"What's wrong with that is she's trying to start a religion!" Linda yelled back.

"I won't be starting a religion this time," Sati remarked, reaching for a cup of water.

"There'll be none of these cults gathering beside my home," Mrs. Hutchinson said indignantly.

Things might have gone on the way they were, or have gotten worse, if my daughter hadn't acted her age upon absorbing the news that God was in the room. Stepping forward, shining with innocence, she offered her flowers to Sati.

"Would you like these?" Jenny asked.

Sati put down her rolling pin and knelt beside Jenny. "Whatever you give me, I will take," she said gently, rubbing a white spot of flour between my daughter's eyebrows. "I'll see you tonight, Jennifer."

The tension suddenly eased, inside and outside. Little girls are good at defusing mobs. Later, I decided, would be time enough to worry about Fred's job and a confused deity. The others appeared to come to a similar conclusion. Mrs. Hutchinson, muttering under her breath, left to finish with her rose bushes. Not looking at Sati, Linda took Jenny's hand and led her out of Fred's claustrophobic apartment. Fred shrugged in my direction and returned to studying the label on the cherries. I knew he'd have a good excuse as to how Sati talked him into distributing the flyers. I would listen to it another time. I went after my family. Sati called goodbye to my back.

Linda was waiting for me in front of the apartments, near her car, pacing the sidewalk. Jenny had returned to helping Mrs. Hutchinson with the flowers.

"Sorry about that, Linda," I said.

She suddenly stopped her fretting, the hardness slipping from her mouth. She laughed. "You sure know how to pick them."

Just like that, just that easy, one friendly line, and I knew I would be thinking about her all day. But I wouldn't wonder why she was with Dick instead of me. I still didn't know how I'd gotten her to marry me in the first place, how I'd talked her into it. She was right, we were meant to go our different ways. She was going to be happy and I was going to be miserable.

"I used up all my luck on my first choice," I said.

Linda hesitated. "That was sweet, Mike."

I gave her a brief kiss on the forehead and turned away. I wanted to end on a nice note. "Have fun today, Linda. I'll see you tonight. Maybe we can go to that meeting together."

I didn't know why I said that.

# Chapter 3

Jenny was glad my car wasn't available, and that we had to go to the bank in my truck. She loved being up high while riding down the road. I'd had an expensive stereo installed to keep me amused on the long road. She always had me crank it up on a heavy metal station. Five years old and she was an Ozzy Osbourne fan. Once I'd suggested to her child psychologist that her favorite music might be related to her nightmares. The dude had smiled; he thought I was old-fashioned.

But today Jenny did not want music. She wanted to talk. "Daddy, Mrs. Hutchinson said the pretty woman was a bad person."

"You mean Sati?"

# Christopher Pike

"Sati," she repeated, apparently liking the sound of the word. "Is she really bad?"

"No. She's just . . . different."

"Why is God different?"

"You mean, why is God indifferent," I said.

"Huh?"

"Never mind." My major in college, before I'd dropped out, had been philosophy, but neither Linda nor I attended church. I had no idea what Jenny was thinking of when she used the word God. "Jenny, Sati isn't God. She's just a person like you and me."

"But she said she was God."

"Jenny, do you know who God is?"

"Yes."

"Who?"

"He's the person who made Santa Claus."

Kids kill me. "OK. Maybe he did make Santa Claus. But if he's a man, you can see how he can't be Sati."

"Why not?"

"Because Sati is a woman."

"But mommy said God can do anything. Why couldn't he be a woman?"

"Hmm. I don't know. I guess you're right. I guess God could be a woman, or a penguin for that matter."

Jenny thought that was funny. "Sati said I could see her tonight. Can I, daddy?"

"We'll see." I paused, remembering my daughter's strange reaction to her. "Why do you want to see her?"

" 'Cause I like her."

30

"Why do you like her? Is it because she's so pretty?"

"Uh-huh. And because she made me happy."

"She made you happy?"

"Uh-huh."

"What did she do that made you happy?" I asked.

"She touched my head."

"Oh."

Banks remind me of dentists' offices. They are wicked places. Evil people work in them. But maybe I have a bad attitude. Seated across from the neatly attired loan officer—with me still in my dirty jeans—I tried to convince myself my paranoia was all in my head.

"I'm afraid we can't grant you the loan, Mr. Winters," the young man said.

"What do you mean?" I asked. Bad news always takes me a while to assimilate. Sometimes I never understand it.

"We can't give you the money," the loan officer said.

Jenny squirmed in the seat beside me. Gesturing for her to be still, I asked, "Why not?"

The young man leaned forward. "You're asking for a hundred and ten thousand dollars to buy two used diesel tractors and two used forty-foot trailers . . ."

"Forty-five-foot trailers, yes?"

"With the intention of using them to hire two new employees and generate twice as much business. Now this seems to be a poor loan for us to make from every angle. First, each of these

31

tractors has over a hundred thousand miles on it."

"They'll go for over three hundred thousand miles."

"Second, you have no written commitment from either of your prospective employees."

"They can't commit until I've got the trucks."

"And third, you have no written commitment from the companies with whom you intend to do business."

"I've given you references from several of my clients," I said. "They have all said they intend to continue to use my partner and myself. Several have stated they would give us considerably more freight if we had the equipment and manpower to handle it."

"But they did not commit," the man insisted. "You have no signed contracts with them."

"That's not the way the trucking business works."

"But it is the way the banking business works, Mr. Winters."

"Are you saying you're not going to give me the money?"

"That's what I said," the man said.

"Oh." It was turning out to be a bad day, I thought. If I had gotten the loan, I could have bought the trucks, and then I could have made a lot more money, and then maybe Linda would have come back to me. "But I've done my banking here for years," I said. "I've never been late with a loan payment. Besides, what's the risk? You have the trucks as collateral. You can always take them away."

The young man pushed my loan application across the desk to me. It had taken me three hours to fill it out. "I'm sorry, Mr. Winters."

"What if I get a cosigner?" I asked.

"Then we will be happy to reconsider the situation."

I stood. "I'll get one right now."

"This afternoon?"

"This minute. Don't go away." I grabbed my daughter's hand. "Come along, Jenny."

David Stone, old buddy and real-estate millionaire, had previously offered to help finance the expansion of my business. I'd not wanted to take him up on the offer, partly because of pride, and partly because even when a friend was involved, business was business with David. I would have to give him a piece of the action. Now I figured I had no choice. I called him at his office from a phone booth outside the bank.

"What's the bank?" he asked when I had explained the situation.

"The First Interstate on Wilshire."

"I know it. What did you say the amount was?" I told him, and it was small change to him. "I'll be through here in an hour, Mike. Could I meet you there at two?"

"I'll be here. I really appreciate this, Dave."

He laughed. "Let's just say when I get into smuggling stuff across the border, I'll be giving you a call. Two o'clock?"

"Right." It wasn't as bad as calling the Godfather, but I wondered after I hung up the phone whether I really needed those extra trucks after all.

Jenny and I had lunch in a coffee shop across the street. Her appointment with the psychologist was approaching. "Jenny, do you want to talk to Dr. McAllister today?"

"Can't I stay with you?" she asked.

I canceled the appointment.

David was almost an hour late. Jenny entertained me by telling me about all the times Dick and Linda fought. I figured that was one relationship on the way out.

David only showed when the bank was about to close. "I got hung up," he said when we met out front. "Did you get the money?"

"What do you mean?"

He laughed, which he did easily and which I suppose was understandable when you were twenty-nine years old and in a position to retire for several lifetimes. He was a thin nervous man with a neat blond moustache and a pointed face that Linda had said was nothing but a big money-sniffing nose, an opinion apparently not shared by the majority of females. Even back in high school, when his means were modest and he couldn't get on an athletic team, David had had lots of girlfriends. He could be charming, when it suited him, and he certainly was sharp. But he had never married. We were more acquaintances than friends.

David had made his money the old-fashioned way: he bought houses for next to nothing from people whose Spanish was excellent, and sold them for a huge profit to people whose first language was Japanese.

"They told me on the phone they would draw up the check for you," he said.

"But don't you have to fill out forms and sign dotted lines?"

He patted Jenny on the head. "How's my girl?"

"Fine," Jenny said, her expression solemn. "But I'm not your girl. You're not my daddy."

David continued, "They trust me, Mike. Let's go inside, you'll see."

David did in fact have to sign a few papers, but he was right about the cashier's check being ready. It felt oddly heavy in my hand, with all those zeros sitting beneath my name. I decided to deposit it immediately. "I can't thank you enough," I said when we were back outside.

"It's no problem," David said.

He wasn't asking for anything in return. I would have to make the offer. "I could pay you a percentage of my profits on the new accounts I get with this money," I said.

David shrugged. "We'll work something out. Hey, want to go down the street for a drink? I know a place that won't hound us about your daughter."

Down the street was five miles away, but riding in David's Ferrari was always fun. When we were seated in a cool dark booth, Jenny with a Coke and David and I with beers, he asked about the chick I'd brought home who thought she was God.

"How did you hear about her?" I asked.

"Hutchinson," David said. "She called me up a few minutes after you left. So what does she look like?"

"Very attractive. Real shiny blond hair, as fine as Jenny's. And she's got these clear blue eyes—you'd have to see them. They're the deepest blue."

"How's the body?"

Jenny was listening to every word. "Looks in good shape," I said.

"Is she totally nuts or what?" David asked.

"If you met her, you'd think she was pretty solid. Her self-confidence is remarkable."

"I'm not surprised, seeing who she believes she is." David sat back. "Think I should stop her from having her meeting?"

"Worried about the other tenants?" I asked.

He nodded. "Hutchinson sounded pretty hot."

"To tell you the truth, Dave, I don't think anyone's going to come."

He considered a moment. "Where did you pick her up?"

"Just past Catson, in the middle of the night."

"Does she have any ID on her?"

"I don't think so. She hasn't got a purse."

"Would you say she's harmless?" David asked.

"Oh, yeah."

"I like her," Jenny said with a note of irritation.

David smiled, then went back to thinking. "If

she's as pretty as you say, we should be able to trace her." He pulled out a pen. "What name is she going by?"

By the time we'd finished another couple of beers, and worked out exactly how much I would pay David for the use of his credit rating, it was close to five. Driving Jenny and me back to my truck, David said he'd let Sati do whatever she wanted, at least for tonight. He also said he'd try to stop by the meeting.

Linda had left a message on my machine, scolding me for canceling Jenny's appointment, and saying she wouldn't be back till eight. Sati was nowhere to be found. I wasn't going to worry about her. Jenny and I decided to take a walk down to the beach. On the way out, we ran into Nick Chevas.

Nick and I had been close in high school, although he hadn't arrived on our campus until his senior year. Before then, he'd lived in east L.A., where he had been a member of a gang. They'd called themselves the Black Bastards, and they'd not been fond of white people, or Hispanics for that matter. Nick hadn't come right out and said it, but from hints he'd dropped, there was blood on his hands, and some of it sounded nasty. Even as a teenager, he'd lifted weights—he could pick me up with one hand without straining.

Two events had helped transform him into a civilized human being. First, his mom, who was the only one he cared about, had had a stroke, followed by a series of heart attacks. There had been no money in the family. He'd nursed her twenty-four hours a day, and as a result, had been forced to give up his violent nocturnal activities. And then when his mother had finally died, the fight in him had apparently died, too. He said it was the first and only time he had cried, and I believed him.

But his mood might have gone bad again, hanging out with the sort he was used to, if his uncle hadn't legally adopted him and moved him into our neighborhood. We met in my garage. I was into being a rock guitarist in those days, and was blasting the block with hard-biting blues when he walked in and said he liked my style. Turned out he could play piano. He had a huge finger spread. We started jamming together right then, and a few months later I got over my fear of being alone with him. At heart, he was really a mellow guy. Except for the four-inch knife scar in front of his left ear, I would have had trouble believing his past.

When people met Nick, they saw that scar first, and I don't suppose many forgot it quickly. He could have been handsome, but when you didn't know him, he just looked mean. He was great with his hands, and had an artistic bent. The art teacher in our high school thought Nick's sketching technique gripping. Unfortunately, his uncle had only agreed to keep him till he was eighteen. Soon after graduation Nick was out on the street again and looking for work everyone was afraid to give him. Finally, he did get a job as a bricklayer. But it was in Oregon, and it was then I lost track of him.

Up north, he learned to construct beautiful fireplaces. Yet he got few of the jobs he bid on. Not many people would let him into their living rooms. He started drinking beer in backwoods bars with people who grew marijuana by the ton in their huge forested backyards. These people were interested in the gang friends Nick had known when he was young. Seemed a few of those friends had since made names for themselves in the drug business. The marijuana farmers wanted Nick to be the go-between for them. Nick was low on cash at the time. It was only marijuana, he thought, and that was hardly a crime anymore. He made it clear he wouldn't handle cocaine, or any hard stuff. The dope planters were agreeable. Nick made the connections with his childhood friends. Deals were struck. Nick started driving a van full of marijuana from Portland to L.A. every week. He became a pusher.

We didn't run into each other again until our ten-year class reunion. It was about this time that Linda started to talk about our psychological incompatibilities. At the reunion, Nick had an illegal alien named Mary Dorado with him. He told me of all the trash he'd been into in the last few years, and how he'd gotten out of it because of Mary. He was poor again, he told me, but his conscience was clear. Mary didn't know he'd ever dealt in dope.

Nick, David, and I got together a week after

the reunion and saw a movie. David told us about his apartments. Nick moved in, with Mary, a couple of weeks later. And six months after that, I moved out of my house and became Nick's upstairs neighbor.

Nick was the only one I told my problems to. He knew how to listen without giving advice, which is a virtue few happy people understand. And he had problems of his own. Mary was pregnant. A good Catholic Hispanic, she wasn't going to have an abortion. She wanted to get married. The timing was bad. Nick had used up all his savings. He was still a mean-looking black dude with a scar. Work was scarce. He'd returned to hauling marijuana, not as much as before, but even a little, he knew, was too much. Mary was getting suspicious. Nick was feeling like dirt.

"How's my babe?" he asked when he saw Jenny. She giggled as he swung her onto his broad shoulders. "How's it going, Mike?"

"My life is a series of ecstatic moments, each more intense than the previous," I said. "How are you?"

"I'm fine," he said without enthusiasm. Jenny began to tickle his ears, and he resettled her atop his head.

"We're walking down to the beach," I said. "Want to come?"

"Sure."

"Mary's welcome, too," I said.

Nick glanced at his apartment door. He looked as tired as I felt. "Her cousin came by and took her shopping. She left a note. She won't be back for a couple of hours."

"You were gone all day?" I asked.

He sighed, setting Jenny down. "Yeah, I was busy."

The beach was only ten minutes away. Once across the Coast Highway and onto the wide stretch of sand leading to the water, Jenny ran on ahead, chasing the pigeons.

"How did it go?" I asked.

He grimaced. "I was coming back down on I-five. I usually bring an extra tank of gas so I don't have to stop at a station. But I forgot this time. You know those jerks up there don't care how they package the stuff. They wrap it in a plastic bag and figure it's cool. But you know how dope smells. You've only got to get close to the van to smell it. Anyway, I end up having to stop near Fresno. Just my luck a cop pulls into the station right then."

"Wonderful."

"Yeah. I thought of just splitting, but his eye went straight to me. He wandered over and started making small talk. Man, I was sweating vinegar. He even leaned his back against my van."

"But you just said how strong it smells?"

Nick laughed. "I was standing there, wondering what kind of fools they have for cops in Fresno, when he starts to tell me about his hay fever. He was suffering something awful with it. His whole head was stuffed up. He couldn't have smelled the dope if he'd stuck his head in a bag full of it. I told him to try alfalfa. My mom used to take that for her allergies. He thanked me for the advice."

"Do you ever feel sometimes that you're tempting the gods?"

Nick lost his smile. "I wasn't laughing about it when I pulled out of the station. I was telling myself that was it."

"Great."

He shook his head. "But when I made my delivery, and got handed a thousand for my troubles, I started thinking maybe I'd make just one last haul. Why is that, Mike?"

"It's because you're an idiot."

Nick nodded. "That's what I need to hear. But I'll tell you, I went out on eight jobs this week. I didn't get a one. And Mary's already seeing this gynecologist that's costing a fortune."

"How far along is she?"

"Ten weeks."

"Is she over her morning sickness?" I asked.

"Yeah, but I think I've caught it."

I took that to mean he wasn't sure he wanted the baby. "Doesn't she ever smell the dope that's been in your van?"

"Sure. I tell her I smoke it occasionally, which I do. She doesn't approve. If only she knew . . ."

"Would she leave you?" I asked.

"I don't like to think about it."

We decided to build Jenny a sand castle. We had a respectable moat in place when Nick got the idea to bury Jenny up to her chin behind the sand walls. I had my doubts. She didn't have on her swimming suit, and the largest waves were already brushing our castle's outer perimeter. I could see Linda freaking out later when she heard about her nightmare-plagued child being buried in front of an advancing tide. But Jenny loved the idea. While Nick dug a hole for her, she pulled her dress off over her head. A few minutes later she was buried so securely that she couldn't budge an inch.

And so we spent until sunset frantically repairing the walls of the castle, with our princess in distress alternately pleading with us to keep her dry, and laughing with us when she got splashed. Finally, however, nature got the best of us. A particularly large foamy wave disintegrated our castle walls in one stroke. Jenny swallowed a mouthful of seawater before we could pull her out. But she giggled all the harder, and I wasn't worried about any psychological trauma.

On the way home, with Jenny again dancing ahead of us, Nick asked me again about my day. I told him about David's cosigning for my loan.

"Must be nice to be rolling in the dough like him," Nick observed.

"When I get the other trucks, I'll be able to offer you a job."

"If you offer it, I'll take it," he said.

"You don't think I'm getting in over my head, do you?"

He looked at me seriously. "You know, Mike, I hate to say this, but I sometimes think I made a mistake talking you into asking Linda to the high school prom."

It hurt—that I was so transparent. He could see why I wanted the loan. And he thought I was wasting my time. "But if you hadn't, we wouldn't have had Jenny to play with today," I said.

"Yeah."

"Look, we're still talking. We're working on it."

"You're working on it. Linda's talking because she wants to be a counselor, and their job is to talk."

I lowered my head. "You're depressing me."

Nick patted me on the back. "Hey, I'm just a dope dealer. What the hell do I know?"

Suddenly, I remembered Sati's meeting. I checked my watch. It was seven-thirty. I was curious what she would have to say, and whether anyone would respond to her flyer.

"Nick, do you want to meet God?" I asked.

"Huh?"

"I've got this girl back at my place who says she's God. Want to hear her talk?"

Nick was interested. "What's she look like?"

"Awesome. Totally awesome."

"Sure."

His reaction did not surprise me. It was, after all, Southern California. Have the right deity and it was a snap to get disciples.

# Chapter 4

Fred met us at the door of my apartment. A glance inside told me someone had been cleaning up. "Sati wants to know if she can use your place for her meeting," he said.

Fred had on dress slacks and a long-sleeved shirt. He'd even washed his face and brushed back his hair. I hardly recognized him. "Tell her if she's God," I said, "she should know whether I'll let her use it or not. Who's been playing housekeeper here?"

"Sati did most of the work. And she said you would let us use the place, but that I should ask you anyway."

Sati had placed my best chair at the end of the room and covered it with a white sheet.

45

Presumably that was where she was going to sit. Roses had been arranged in a vase on the corner table beside the chair.

"But the flyer directed them to your place," I said.

"I'm to wait down there and direct them up here."

"She told you that?"

"Yeah," Fred said. "And I know what you're going to say, that I shouldn't listen to her because she's crazy."

"Well, now that you mention it."

Fred lowered his voice and spoke confidentially. Nick, who was carrying Jenny, had to lean closer to hear. "I spent the whole day with her," Fred said. "I've never seen anyone like her. *Everything* goes her way. We went to the bank on Third Street to see if we could use their community room for another meeting she wants to hold tomorrow night. We talked to the bank president. At first he said we had to meet all these conditions: we had to be a registered nonprofit society; we had to fill out an application; we had to make reservations a month in advance—all this crap. But then she just started talking to him, telling him she was God, and that she needed the room tomorrow. And he gave it to her!"

"I've got to see this woman," Nick said.

"You'll like her," Jenny reassured him.

"He gave her the room because she's pretty and charming," I said. "I knew her two minutes and bought her breakfast. It doesn't mean a thing."

Fred wasn't convinced. "She's got something, Mike. I don't know what it is, but it's something."

The glint in his eyes had me concerned. "Have you seen Linda?" I asked.

"Yeah," Fred said. "She was here a moment ago. She went out looking for you. What about Sati using your apartment?"

"Tell her . . . what the hell, tell her OK."

Nick went downstairs to see if Mary had returned. Fred headed for his apartment. I went searching for clothes for Jenny. I'd only gotten her into a fresh pair of pants when David Stone and Mrs. Hutchinson appeared in the doorway.

"Fred told us this was the place," David said.

I smiled. "Welcome to the ashram. I'm surprised to see you here, Mrs. Hutchinson."

She scowled. "Someone's got to stand up against this nonsense. That girl's got her whole life in front of her. I'm not going to let her throw it away. I'm going to give her a good talking-to, and she's going to listen."

A few minutes later, a young couple showed up. They looked and acted completely normal. All they asked was if this was where the meeting was to be held. I might have struck up a conversation with them, and inquired if they didn't have a better way to spend their Monday night, when a mother and teenaged daughter appeared, followed quickly by a middle-aged man. Incredibly, none of the people appeared unusual. It was now minutes before eight o'clock.

Linda poked her head inside the door. "Is this really happening?" she asked.

The group glanced at her, and the mother and daughter fidgeted slightly. Jenny had taken a seat on the floor near Sati's chair. She hardly noticed Linda's entrance. I ushered Linda onto my patio.

"Why not stay?" I asked. "Jenny's been looking forward to seeing Sati all day."

To my amazement, Linda did not protest. "As long as she isn't kept up too late. Did she give you any trouble?"

"No," I said. "I got the loan."

Linda smiled, but it was a polite reflex. And all the hassle with the bank was aimed at getting her back, I thought. "I'm glad," she said.

Nick returned. He said Mary was still out. Since our guests had already monopolized the couch, the three of us decided to take a seat against the wall farthest from the sheet-draped chair. Fred reappeared a moment later and joined Jenny on the floor up front.

At precisely eight o'clock, Sati entered.

She had changed. Her dress was no different, and she was wearing her hair the same as when I had picked her up, loose over her shoulders. Her serene expression was also as I remembered. Yet it was as though I were seeing her for the first time. I did not know why that was so.

Taking a seat on the covered chair, she slowly scanned the room, her big eyes lingering for several seconds on each person. I was the last one she came to, and with me she smiled. I found myself holding my breath, and had to consciously tell myself to exhale.

"We will start with a few minutes of silence with eyes closed," she said, addressing the group. "During these few minutes, do not mind how you feel or what you're thinking. Just be comfortable. I will signal when to open your eyes." She resettled herself in her chair and folded her hands in her lap. "Close your eyes."

Normally, I consider myself a relaxed person, though there is always the odd spell when I can't sit still. When Sati told us to close our eyes, I feared I was in for one of those times. All of a sudden, the last thing I wanted to do was be motionless. It was like someone had sprinkled an itchy powder directly onto my nervous system. A couple of minutes of this went by. I considered getting up and leaving.

Then something unexpected happened. Just when I thought I couldn't sit there a moment more, I began to relax. But it was much more than simple relaxation. A delicious warmth started to spread from my chest while, paradoxically, a cool current began to flow across my forehead. Both sensations were remarkably pleasant. As my attention went to them, I noticed the muscles along my spine twitching, letting go. Pretty soon I was so comfortable I was sure I was going to fall asleep. Yet quite the opposite happened.

My mind started to float, yet my thoughts drifted past with crystal clarity. It was as if I could see them, as if they were somehow separate from myself. The question of what was happening to me also floated by, but not the answer, and I really didn't care. I felt I could sit there forever and ever.

Sati spoke. Her voice seemed to come from far off. How perfect it sounded to me right then, despite the fact that she was interrupting my peace. Soft and deep, rich with a young girl's sweetness. She was telling us to open our eyes. I did as requested.

Everyone in the room appeared to have been as settled as I was. Linda was having trouble getting her eyelids to stay up. She turned my way, and I could have sworn the last ten years had never happened to her. There wasn't a line on her face.

"Did I fall asleep?" she whispered.

"Did you?" I asked.

She frowned, checking her watch. "I must have. A half hour's gone by."

I had to check my own watch to believe her. Sleep must have caught me unaware, too, I decided. Sitting on the other side of Linda, Nick smiled and shook his head, equally amazed at the passage of time.

"Thank you all for coming," Sati began. "This will be the first time I have spoken publicly, and for that reason, tonight is special for all of us."

She paused, again carefully taking in everyone in the room. A solitary corner lamp was the room's only source of light. Her blue eyes sparkled through the dimness. "My name is Sati. It is a name none of you consciously recognize, an ancient name you may translate as the word *God*. I am God. But I am not the one you imagine when you think the word *God*. I am beyond your imagination and your thoughts. My nature is divine. It is indescribable; therefore, I will shy away from words while I describe it to you. I say 'shy' for I know in the days to come we will inevitably exchange many words. Such is your state that you depend almost exclusively upon words for understanding. But do not feel belittled by my last comment. You are all great. You are all divine. You are the same as myself. Just now you caught a faint glimpse of yourself, and almost saw me. When I talk, I talk to myself. There is only one of us here."

She grinned, even laughed a little, and I noticed she was tugging on her hair. "But if none of this has meaning to you, accept me as a girl. I *am* a girl, a very young one at that. I like to play. You will ask why I am here, what profound purpose my coming foretells. You will be disappointed to hear I have no particular purpose in coming. I am here because it suits me to be here. This world, this entire creation, is my playground. I made it to play in, for you to find delight in. The purpose of your lives is to expand my joy, which is already infinite. Can you honestly imagine any other reason for being here?"

She plucked a rose from the vase and began

to caress the petals. "Still, I know you will want a message from me. When I'm asked a question, I find it difficult not to answer. I *do* hear your prayers. And if you listen closely right now, you will receive all the spoken wisdom from this girl that you are going to receive. But do not feel you have to believe what I say. I don't ask for your belief. I never ask anything from anybody.

"You were not born to suffer. If, in spite of what I tell you now, you choose to be miserable, then you do so for your own sake, not for mine. There is hardly a religious or mystical tradition in the world that does not describe God as eternal bliss. This being so, why should anyone suffer for God? It makes no sense. Therefore, my first and deepest wish for all of you is to be happy. Just that simple—be happy.

"On the other hand, I do understand that you all suffer, to one extent or another. I will tell you why. You have lost the awareness of the two sides of my nature, of your nature. I am silent and I am active. I am both simultaneously. You are both, too, but you experience only your active side. You have forgotten your inner being, which is pure silence. You search endlessly for permanent happiness in a place where nothing is permanent. Here I am getting philosophical, and that is a shame because truth is always very simple. There is a state that you as a human being can aspire to that includes an awareness of both sides of my nature, a state beyond all sorrow. Call it what you will. Your oldest traditions give it many names. 'Sati' is one of them.

"Enjoy your life. No curse hangs over you, nor did it ever. No devil chases after your soul. Sing and dance and be merry. But in your play, remember that the goal of the game—and there is a goal—is to find me. How you reach this goal, I will not tell you. I respect your free will, and I do so love a good drama, although I begin to tire of the tragedies you continue to play. Don't simply knock and wait for the door to be opened. Go look for the keys. Some fit the lock better than others."

Sati stopped and smelled the rose. "I am through lecturing for tonight. I won't be taking questions. But I will be giving another talk tomorrow night at eight o'clock. It will take place in the community room of the bank on the corner of Third and Wilshire. Feel free to come, and if you wish, bring your family and friends. Now we will close with a minute of silence. And before you leave, have some of my cookies. This girl spent half the day baking them." She nodded. "Close your eyes."

This time she meant a minute when she said it. I had scarcely begun to settle when she stopped me. What was interesting was that I had even begun to relax at all in so short a time. There was a vibe in the room that was sucking me into myself. I was dumbfounded.

The cookies were excellent. Tiny shortbread cakes, they had raspberry jam in the center and icing and sliced cherry pieces on top. I ate half a dozen.

The group left slowly. Leaning against the back wall with Linda and Nick and munching on the goodies, I watched as the people went up to Sati and introduced themselves. They mainly thanked her for her lecture and her "meditation." I hadn't even known we were meditating. She shook each of their hands and beamed when they told her how peaceful they had felt while sitting with their eyes shut. My amazement continued to grow.

"Did she hypnotize us or what?" Nick asked.

"She didn't plant any suggestions before she had us close our eyes," I said.

"Not verbally, you mean," Linda said, watching as Jenny stayed close to Sati's side. "Her body language is extremely suggestive of easiness and relaxation."

"Then you felt relaxed?" I asked.

Linda shrugged. "I usually do when I sit with my eyes closed."

"I've never felt that relaxed," Nick said. "Not even when I've been stoned."

David also thanked Sati for her talk. As he was leaving, he gestured to me. "Could I have a word with you outside, Mike?"

"Sure," I said.

We stopped in front of the apartments beside his Ferrari. The night was warm and clear, with a gentle salty breeze coming from the ocean. "That girl's the most incredible person I've ever seen in my life," David said with feeling.

"You liked her talk that much?"

"Who cares about her talk? It's the way she handles herself that gets me. What charisma! What a face! That girl's going places."

"If you believe what she says, she's already been everywhere."

"I'm serious, Mike. I want you to keep her around. Don't let her get away. I know what, I'll give her an apartment for free."

"But they're all taken," I said.

"Oh, yeah. Well, keep her at your place."

"But what if she doesn't want to stay at my place?"

"Make her comfortable. Feed her and flatter her. Just keep your eye on her."

"But why?"

David was getting impatient. "You saw the way those people reacted to her. She's got something."

I paused. "Fred said that."

"You should listen to him. There's magic there, I can feel it."

"So?"

"So we can't let it get away."

"Dave, we can't tell her what to do."

"We're not. We're just helping her out. You're the one who said she didn't have a purse or any money. What's wrong with taking care of her?" He slapped me on the arm. "Besides, how can you complain about sleeping in the same place as her?"

"If she wants to stay for a few days, that would be fine with me. But I'm going to let her

make up her own mind. From what I've seen of
her, she's going to do that, anyway."

David wasn't satisfied with my attitude. He
started to get in his car. "Thanks for inviting me
tonight, Mike."

"Coming tomorrow?" I asked.

"You can count on it. Good night."

Linda and Jenny met me near the pool as I
walked back to my place. At that moment, the
young couple who had shown up first waved to
us as they went out the back way. They were
both smiling.

"They had fun," I observed.

Linda was swinging Jenny in her arms. "This
little girl has had too much fun today. She told
me how you buried her at the beach."

"Nick made me do it." Linda wasn't mad
about it, which surprised me. But not nearly as
much as did the envelope she pulled out of her
back pocket. She handed it to me.

"I know you told me to mail it to you, but this
way you get it a day less late." She gave me a
quick kiss on the lips. "Happy birthday, Mike."

It was just a store-bought birthday card—an
undistinguished one at that—but for me it put a
pleasant finish to the evening. "I hope it doesn't
shrink when I wash it," I gushed.

"You don't wash it, daddy," Jenny said. "You
put it in the drawer."

I messed up my daughter's hair. "Did you like
Sati's meeting?"

"Uh-huh."

"Didn't you want to get up and walk around

when we were all sitting with our eyes closed?"
I asked.

"I had my eyes closed, too!"

"But didn't you feel bored?"

Jenny didn't understand how I could be so
dense. "I was happy. I want to sit with Sati lots
of times."

"Where will Sati be staying tonight?" Linda
asked.

"Probably at my place."

Had I been hoping for a sign of jealousy, I
would have been disappointed. But my expectations were more realistic than that. Despite
her outburst that afternoon about me bringing
a blond home to play with, Linda wanted me
dating.

"That's nice," she said. "Keep in touch."

"Of course," I said.

I ran into Nick and Fred going up my stairs.
Fred was excited. He appeared to have infected
Nick.

"Mary just got home," Nick said. "I've got to
tell her about this girl. Going to be around
tomorrow?"

I shook my head. "I've got a load to pick up
early and take to Phoenix."

Nick headed for his door. "See you Wednesday, then. Take care of yourself."

When he was gone, Fred laughed. "Convinced,
Mike?"

"Of what?"

"Come off it! She's got incredible vibes. I saw

you when we opened our eyes that first time. She'd zapped you, too."

"Somehow, I never pictured God going around zapping people. Jesus didn't do that in the Bible."

"I bet he did."

And just this morning Fred had taken everything I said as gospel. We could argue about it later, I decided. I nodded toward my wide-open door. "Is Sati done visiting with the people?" I asked.

"Yeah, except for Mrs. Hutchinson."

"Swell."

Fred wasn't worried. "Sati can handle her. I can't wait until tomorrow. I'm going to bring Lori. I told Sati about her and she wants to meet her."

"Did you get your car fixed?"

Fred nodded absently. "Yeah. It was the battery cable."

"Burned out?"

"No, it had fallen off. I better get to bed, Mike."

"Since when do you go to bed before midnight?"

He yawned. "Sati told me to go rest."

"That sounds like good motherly advice."

Upstairs, Mrs. Hutchinson was hammering on Sati, for all the good it was doing.

"You're such a pretty and intelligent girl," Mrs. Hutchinson was saying. "You could do almost anything. Why are you wasting your life going around spouting nonsense? You're not just deceiving people, you know, you're committing a sin against our Lord."

"Don't worry about me," Sati said. "I'll be fine."

"But what you're saying is atrocious! It violates scripture!"

Sati was patient. "You're a good person. I know you wish me the best. But your concerns are misdirected. Go and rest now. Tomorrow, you will come to the meeting, and things will become clearer for you." She raised her hand as Mrs. Hutchinson went to blast her again. "Enough said, Carol. Go to bed."

Mrs. Hutchinson froze for a moment, then did as she was told. She stalked past me. The great vibes apparently hadn't infected everyone, I thought. I hadn't known her first name was Carol.

Sati hardly seemed to know I was there. Taking a seat on the couch, I watched as she stared off into empty space for a full minute. In that time, she didn't blink once. I wasn't even sure if she breathed. Finally, she said, "Michael, you're coming to the meeting, too."

"I'm afraid that's impossible. I have to go to Phoenix." I pulled my schedule book from a drawer in the coffee table. "See, I have to pick up a load of books in the valley tomorrow and deliver them in Phoenix."

Sati plucked the schedule from my hands and studied it. "There is a Jesse written here. Is he scheduled tomorrow?"

"Jesse's my partner. Well, I call him that. He's

actually more of an employee. He has tomorrow off."

"He has your other truck?"

I had to assume Fred had told her I had two of them. "Yeah."

Sati closed the schedule book, her expression still far away. "You need to rest," she said.

"Yeah, I was thinking of turning in soon. I have to be up at four. You can have the bedroom. I don't mind the couch."

"You will sleep in your own room."

"But I'll be getting up early. I'll wake you."

"I will be up before you," she said.

"But you've been going since I picked you up. You must be exhausted."

"I am never tired."

"But you do sleep?"

"I rest."

"Did you get something to eat this evening?" I'd forgotten dinner, myself.

"I'll eat tomorrow. Go to bed, Michael. Your body needs to assimilate what you experienced tonight."

"What did I experience?"

Sati looked at me closely. "The experience explains itself. Words don't explain it."

Her seriousness did not make me uncomfortable. Indeed, it struck me then that for someone I hardly knew—someone who could at best be described as unusual—I felt totally at ease with her.

"But you still think of yourself as a person,

don't you?" I said. "You said tonight you were a girl."

She nodded. "I am a girl."

"Do you have parents?"

"No."

"Did you ever have parents?"

"I am self-born. This body you see came into being four days ago in the desert, near where you met me."

That was quite a statement. "What were you doing out there before I came along?"

She touched my outstretched knee. "I was waiting for you."

"Why me?"

"There is a reason for everything."

"Are you going to tell me what it is?"

She squeezed my leg and let go. "Not tonight."

"When?"

"Before I leave."

"When are you going to leave?"

"When this body dies."

# Chapter 5

When I awoke, I knew immediately I wasn't going to Phoenix that day. The sun was streaming through my open window at a steep angle, which it did not do at four in the morning. A glance at the clock told me I had overslept *six* hours. It was five after ten. I felt behind the clock and discovered the alarm switch pressed in. I knew for a fact I had pulled it out before going to sleep.

There was a note taped on the inside of my bedroom door, printed in neat ink letters on a piece of notebook paper.

Michael,
    Jesse picked up the books and is on his way to Phoenix.

                                        Sati

I wasn't mad. I felt too refreshed to be mad. It had probably been the best night's sleep I'd had since I was ten years old. Also, I should have seen it coming. Jesse's number had been listed in the schedule book, and Sati had made a point of the fact that Jesse was going to be available.

She was nowhere to be found. In the bathroom, I discovered a slightly damp towel and a few strands of long blond hair in the bathtub. So our resident Goddess did get dirty and shed her hair, I thought.

The only available shampoo was in a brandnew bottle that Sati had not troubled to open. But turning on the water, I had to wonder if she hadn't used some kind of soap. The tub smelled faintly of honey.

When I came out of the shower, I found Mary Dorado, Nick's girlfriend, knocking on the front door. She had a huge box of clothes in her hands. Because she was pregnant, I immediately snatched it out of her hands. I had treated Linda the same way when she was carrying Jenny. And of course it had irritated her.

"This is heavy, Mary," I said. "You shouldn't have carried it up the stairs. What's it for, anyway?"

"Sati."

Mary and Sati had similar bodies. I glanced in the box. "These look like your best clothes."

Mary nodded. She did not talk a lot, although not for the obvious reason. Despite being an illegal alien and having been in the country less than a year, her English was excellent. She was just, in Nick's word, "respectful." She had been born in a tiny village in Nicaragua, and had left with her mother and two sisters when her father had been "accidentally" killed by soldiers. Who these soldiers were, Contras or Nicaraguan military personnel, was not clear. I suppose it didn't really matter. Mary had made her way north over a period of six months. She was now a seamstress in a shop owned by the same people Mrs. Hutchinson had worked for. Like so many other illegal aliens in Southern California, she lived in fear of being caught by an immigration official. Poor Nick, he had a lot of reasons why he had to marry her.

"Where is she?" I asked, motioning Mary inside, happy for the clothes. The previous night, I had offered Sati a pair of shrunken sweats to sleep in. I didn't know if she had used them.

"Mrs. Hutchinson is showing her parts of the Bible," Mary said.

"Have a seat on the couch. Really? That would be fun to watch. I take it Sati is holding her own."

"Yes."

"Would you like something to drink?"

"No, thank you." Mary sat down. "Sati told me to tell you she would be making you breakfast."

I laughed and pulled up a chair across from Mary. "I haven't had anyone make me breakfast since, why, the last time you made it for me. I hope she's half as good a cook." Mary blushed shyly. I went on, "Have you spoken to Sati much?"

Mary nodded. "She invited me to walk with her."

"Where did you go?"

"To the beach."

"Just the two of you?"

"Yes."

"What do you think of her?"

Mary hesitated, her serious face tensing slightly. "She is . . . I don't have the right words. She is like someone my mother once took me to when I was a little girl and very sick."

"A healer?"

Mary nodded. "I had a fever, and the doctor was far away at another village. This man put his hand on my forehead and I was better."

"Did Sati touch you?"

"No."

"Then why does she remind you of this healer?"

"She can heal. Mrs. Hutchinson's fingers are already better."

I sat up. "What do you mean?"

A light glittered in Mary's usually soft eyes. "She has been working in her garden all morning. She is weeding and turning the soil with both hands."

"Does Mrs. Hutchinson know Sati's healed her?"

Mary shook her head.

"Why not?" I asked.

"She says only God can heal."

"But does she know her hands are better?"

"She should," Mary said.

My heart was pounding and I was glad Mary could not hear it. My reaction to the news embarrassed me. Arthritis was the one disease faith healers were famous for improving. Lay on the hands, I thought, invoke the name of the Lord, and practically any desperate person would start bending parts that hadn't moved in a while.

Except Sati had done neither of the above. She had told no one what to expect from her period of silence. And Mrs. Hutchinson had not come to her for healing.

"Mary, you're Catholic," I said. "Doesn't it bother you that Sati says she's God?"

"Holy people can be strange. Saint Francis used to run naked with the animals."

"Then you think she's a saint?"

Mary nodded. "You can see it in her eyes, and hear it in her words."

"But she's not even Catholic."

Mary shifted uneasily. "She could be baptized."

Sati walked in at that moment and all thoughts of miracles went out the window. Her white dress was gone. In its place was a tight red T-shirt and a baggy pair of white running shorts. The absence of a bra created an interesting effect, with her shiny hair hanging around her breasts. Her legs were tanned, even slightly sunburned.

"You were talking about me," she said with a

laugh. In that moment, I imagined she was a college coed back from cheerleading practice. The serene power that had seemingly emanated from her the previous night was hard to find.

"No, we were discussing running with animals," I stammered, imagining how *she* would look in place of crazy Francis. I also thought if this really was God I would be going straight to hell the second I died.

Sati smiled. "I don't believe you."

I could feel the blood in my face. "In that case, am I forgiven for lying to you?"

"Certainly. I forgive everybody everything, even when they don't ask for forgiveness." She turned toward the kitchen. "What do you want for breakfast?"

"Don't you know?" I teased.

"Pancakes," Sati said. "You want pancakes."

"You're wrong. I was thinking of having bacon and sausage."

"There is no bacon or sausage in the icebox. Besides, when you taste my pancakes, you'll realize they're what you really wanted."

Her pancakes were excellent, better than Pete's at the diner. Not long afterward, Sati sat beside me in the kitchen as I shoved them hungrily into my mouth, her bare legs tucked cross-legged beneath her, fine golden hairs just visible from the top of her thighs to her ankles. She didn't shave her legs, I noted, and there wasn't a male on the planet who would have minded.

Mary had returned home. I was sort of glad.

It was nice to have Sati to myself for a few minutes.

"Have you had breakfast?" I asked, reaching for the butter.

"I wanted to have breakfast with you."

"Then what are you waiting for?" I nodded to the steaming food stacked on the plate in the center of the table. "Eat."

It was as if she had been waiting to make sure I was taken care of. Fetching another plate, she lifted two small pancakes for herself.

"Is that all you're having?" I asked.

"It is enough for me."

I stood. "I forgot the milk."

"I should get it for you."

"No problem," I said, already at the icebox. There were two opened cartons inside. I took the closest one. Returning to the table, I poured us each a full glass. Sati stared at her glass for a moment, but I didn't pay it any heed. She was always staring at things.

"What time did you turn off my alarm and call Jesse?" I asked.

"Clever boy. Four in the morning. He was glad for the extra work. I told him you would pay him double."

I almost choked on my milk. "Why did you tell him that?"

"I had just woken him up. I didn't want him mad at me."

"Did he ask who you were?"

Sati nodded. "He's coming to one of my meetings this week."

69

Jesse was a conservative fellow. She must have given him a great pitch. "Are you going to have lots of them?" I asked.

"Every night."

"Are you going to do any advertising?"

"Word of mouth will be enough."

"But you'd reach a lot more people if you put out some ads."

"Numbers are not as important as you think."

"You're not trying to reach everyone?"

"When I reach one, I reach everyone. There is only one of us here."

"You?"

"And you."

The telephone rang. "Hello?" I said with a full mouth.

"Michael, what are you doing home?" Linda asked.

"Eating pancakes," I said. "What's up?"

"It's Jenny. She was up half the night with horrible dreams. I wanted to take her to McAllister, but she says she'll only talk to Sati. I'm worried about her. Is Sati there?"

"Yes." I put my hand over the phone. "My daughter's been having nightmares for months now. She had them last night. She wants to talk to you."

Sati drank her milk. "Have Linda bring her here."

"You don't want to just talk to her on the phone?"

"No."

I spoke to Linda. "Sati says to bring her here."

Linda did not protest, and that worried me. Jenny must have been extremely upset.

I said goodbye to Linda and put down the phone. "I slept so well last night," I muttered. "When I first woke up, I honestly thought your meeting last night had something to do with it."

"You're disappointed that the silence did not help your daughter?"

"I'm not looking for miracles, Sati."

She was doubtful. "But you would like to see one. Something you could verify with your senses. I'll give you none of those. You'll recognize me from inside yourself, or you won't recognize me at all."

"But Mary says you've healed Mrs. Hutchinson's arthritis. Is that true?"

"The rest during the silence last night has helped her condition."

"I don't see how simple rest could get her fingers working again."

"Rest is a great gift. It is the silent side of my nature. When it is perfect, it can heal anything."

"How did you do . . . whatever it was you did last night?"

"Why ask? You don't think I did anything." She smiled. "Your doubts don't bother me. Deep inside, you know who I am."

"But I don't know it consciously?"

"Yes."

"Then what good does it do me? Sati, I don't want to strain our friendship, especially after you've gone to all the trouble to make me breakfast, but I don't think you're God. You're asking too much."

"Did I ask for your belief?"

"I assumed you wanted it."

"Your happiness is what I want. I am a God of bliss; a happy man does me the greatest worship just by being alive."

"All right." I returned to my pancakes. "But I think I'd be a lot happier if I knew my daughter was all right."

"My touch can be cool and soothing. It can also burn, if the need is there. The experience of silence caused Jennifer's avalanche of dreams. But it is good. They will pass and she will feel better."

"I sure hope so."

We finished our breakfast and together did the dishes. I thought I should use my unexpected free time to take another look at the tractors and trailers I was planning on buying. But I ended up sitting in the living room with Sati. She was not an easy person to leave. *This* I did realize consciously.

We had not been talking long when Timmy Pinton came to the door. Timmy also lived in the apartments, across the swimming pool from my place. The day I'd moved in, he'd helped me unload my furniture. But he wouldn't be helping me load it back on the truck if Linda ever had a change of heart and wanted to give the marriage another shot. He was forty pounds lighter than he had been last November. He was a thirty-five-year-old homosexual with AIDS. Next to Nick, he was the best friend I had.

When I opened the door, the sight of him almost brought tears to my eyes. With my busy schedule, I'd missed him the last couple of weeks, and it seemed he had shrunk even more in that short time. His once thick auburn hair was so thin I knew it must come out in handfuls when he showered, the side effect of some new wonder drug. His generous hello smile did not help—I could see every bone in his face. It was amazing he could still get around. He'd had a cough for the last two months.

"Mike," he said. "You look like you just saw a ghost."

"How are you doing, Timmy?" I asked, trying to sound casual.

"Wonderful. Got a great story for you. I was down at the drugstore getting a prescription filled, when this redneck dude—he looked like one of you gorgeous truck drivers—asked what was ailing me. He sounded sort of suspicious so I told him I had a brain tumor, and that I was buying medicine to help with the pain. Little did I realize the poor sap's mom had died of a brain tumor. Anyway, he felt so guilty and all that, he offered to buy me an ice cream next door.

"We were sitting there, enjoying our cones, talking about what a bitch life can be, when these two old boyfriends walk by on the sidewalk. They were holding hands. They didn't see me but the truck driver saw them, and said something about AIDS, and the plagues in Revelations, and how it's about time the scum got washed away. Naturally, I asked if I could have a taste of his cone. Ordinarily he probably wouldn't have let me have a bite, but he must have gotten to thinking about his mom and feeling nostalgic. 'Sure, son,' he said, and I took this big slurpy lick. Then we talked some more, and ate some more ice cream. Finally these two old pals of mine reappeared, walking in the other direction on the sidewalk. Before the guy could say anything again, I jumped up and shouted, 'Hey, I know those dudes! They're my buddies!'"

Timmy giggled. "You should have been there, Mike. He looked down at his ice cream with these big bulging eyes. You'd have sworn he was going to vomit. I thought of giving him a lecture on how you can't get AIDS from someone's ice-cream cone, but I don't think he would have believed me."

"You didn't tell him you had AIDS?" I asked.

"That's what made it so perfect. I didn't have to. He *knew*."

"I'm surprised he didn't kill you."

Timmy chuckled. "He was afraid to touch me."

I patted him on the back. "Glad to see you're having fun. But why are we doing all this talking here? Come on in." I stepped aside and let him pass, his eyes lighting the instant he saw Sati. She was sitting cross-legged on the couch. "I have a visitor you might have heard of," I said. "Sati, this is Timmy. He lives in apartment eight. Timmy, this is Sati. She's . . . someone I met."

Sati nodded, not budging from her seat. "Hello, Timothy."

"Oh, you're nice," he said, immediately swooping over to sit beside her. "Is it true what they say about you?"

"By 'they' do you mean the Moslems or the Jews?" she asked.

We all laughed together. I took a seat across from them. Timmy boldly touched her bare knee. "Why did you come as a blond this time?" he asked.

If he was trying to intimidate her with his nearness, he was not succeeding. "It is you who determine how I will look," she said.

"But I had a strong black dude in mind for my Second Coming," Timmy said.

"I was speaking of the group desire of the human race." She smiled and patted his arm. "But maybe next time."

"Then you'll be coming again after this?" I asked.

"Yes," she said. "There are many comings. Time is much older than any of you imagine. I never leave you lost and rolling in its waves for long."

"Why leave us lost at all?" Timmy asked, easing back into the couch. I knew he had come

75

strictly to joke with her, but he appeared to be having second thoughts.

"Yes," I said. "Why all this suffering when we're supposed to be happy all the time? Or are you going to say our suffering is only an illusion?"

She shook her head. "You feel pain, do you not? It must have some reality. But I can't satisfy your question with words. The only true answer is to realize your inner self. Then this question and all paradoxes associated with life will disappear."

"How about telling us a parable?" Timmy suggested. "Jesus did all right with those."

Sati tugged on her hair. "Very well. But an analogy will serve us better than a parable." She considered for a moment. "When you are sitting still in a hot bath, it sometimes happens, if you sit long enough, that you no longer feel the warmth. You have to wiggle a toe to feel it. Then you say to yourself, 'Yes, this warmth is delightful.' You see, I am always complete, always warm. But occasionally I have the desire to feel my warmth." She gestured above. "All this vast creation is a ripple from when I wiggled my toe. Each of you is an infinitesimal bubble created by that ripple. You float in my waters, surrounded by my waters, yet you are always dry inside, always looking for a drink. Until the day your bubble pops, and you are me again."

"The individual bubbles represent individual souls?" I asked.

"Yes."

"But why did you make us dry?" Timmy asked.

Sati looked at him strangely. "Who ever heard of a bubble full of water?" Then she began to laugh. She laughed so hard, we were forced to join her.

"But you still haven't answered the question," I said after a bit. "Why did you have us make bubbles at all? Why not sponges? Then we could have stayed wet and warm and still had room for air spaces."

"But I made sponges," Sati said, red-faced, trying to catch her breath from her outburst. "I made angels."

"There are really angels?" Timmy asked.

"Oh, yes."

"Male and female ones?"

"Definitely."

He smiled. "Are any of them gay?"

"They're all celibate."

Timmy was disappointed. "How dull."

"I wouldn't say that," she replied. "You should see how wild they get at choir practice."

"But last night you said there was a reason for everything," I said, trying for a third time to have my question answered. "I've really wondered about this suffering thing all my life."

Sati began to speak, to laugh, then fell silent, holding my eyes. I could wax on forever about the clarity of her eyes, the way the blue seemed to shine no matter what the lighting. But I would just keep saying the same thing.

Sati had a window at her back, and the sun was warm and soft through her long hair, with the rays also touching the whole of my right arm and part of my right leg. I forget the name of it now, but I once saw a Woody Allen film, where the main character—played by Woody Allen—spoke of a single golden instant in his relationship with a woman. The beauty of the moment lay in its simplicity. His girlfriend was reading her paper in the morning and she just looked up at him and smiled. And everything—life, love, the world—was perfect for the character.

I felt that way in that moment, with Sati looking at me.

It wasn't by any stretch of the imagination an overwhelming experience. I did not feel the depth of the silence I had the previous night. But I was completely at ease. For a few seconds, I couldn't imagine anything I would rather be doing, any place I would rather be. The sun on the skin of my arm was a delight. Sati continued to look at me without blinking, and I believe she knew exactly how I felt. It was only then that I wondered if this was not the mystical state she had spoken of earlier, if it wasn't something as natural as sitting and enjoying the sun in the company of friends.

Perhaps because of my state of mind, what she said next went deep inside. It was a comment that was to stay with me always, and come to me whenever I tried to figure out things I should have known enough to leave alone.

"You say you wonder, Michael," Sati said. "That is good. There is a difference between a question and a wonder. I would prefer to answer only questions that will be of benefit to you. A child looks up at the starry sky at night and wonders. He is filled with the joy of the mystery of creation. That is a wonderful thing. Why should I explain everything to you and take away that joy? I will not. The purpose of my words is to create silence, to create joy. I am not here to stuff your head full of knowledge. A child starts out innocent. You ask him something and he says, 'I don't know.' Then that child grows up and thinks he knows everything. I'll teach you something, both of you. I'll teach you to say 'I don't know,' and be glad. That is true knowledge."

I heard her. I really did. And I thought about what she had said before I spoke next. But maybe that was the problem. Maybe I shouldn't have thought about it. Maybe I should have kept my mouth shut and continued to enjoy the sun on my arm and the blue in her eyes. Certainly, the moment I opened my mouth, the spell was broken.

"I just thought you might be able to throw some light on the dilemma," I said, adding sheepishly, "that was the only reason I asked."

"Then I will, if that is what you really want." Sati paused again. "Reality is different in different states of consciousness. Ordinarily you know three states in daily life: waking, dreaming, and sleeping." She gestured about the room. "When you're awake, you see this chair here, that table there. And it is real to you. No one who was awake could argue with that. But say you go to sleep on this couch. You fall into a deep slumber. Then as far as you know, this room doesn't even exist. Nothing exists. Now say you begin to dream of living in a palace. Suddenly the walls of this room are transformed into tall white pillars draped with golden silk. Nothing has changed, only your state of consciousness, yet everything has changed."

"But what we experience when we're asleep or dreaming isn't real," I said.

"But what you experience when you're awake is real?" Sati asked.

"Absolutely," I said.

Sati nodded. "Very good. It is real. It is real for that state of consciousness. And it would be foolish to pretend that one is in another state of consciousness when one isn't. That is the problem you have today with so much of what is written and said about higher states of consciousness. People make moods about being in cosmic consciousness or nirvana consciousness. They pretend to be someone they're not. Practical people see this and don't want to have anything to do with the whole business. The ultimate reality can't be understood from the waking state any more than this room could be appreciated by an unconscious man. But as I said last night, there are other states, states as far above waking as waking is above sleeping. They are real. They can be experienced. And in those states, there is no question of suffering. There are no questions, period. There is only me."

"Are you in one of these higher states?" Timmy asked.

"Yes," Sati said. "The very highest. There is nothing higher than me."

"How would you know for sure that you are?" I asked. "How can you be sure it's not just a powerful mood?"

"There's a difference in the working of the body," Sati said.

"Huh?" I said.

Sati raised an eyebrow, playing with me. "You wonder about this?"

"I'd like to know," I said.

"I'll talk about it tonight at the meeting."

"What's wrong with right now?" I asked.

Sati shrugged. "People will ask about this. You will see. I will talk. Be patient."

"But what about the bubbles in the tub?" Timmy asked. "Let's get back to those."

"Oh, eventually they pop," Sati said. "Then there is only God. There is only me." She grinned. "And the bathtub feels *so* warm, and now it remembers that it was *always* warm."

"You mean, eventually everybody gets to take a bath with you?" Timmy asked, interested.

Sati was amused. "Yes."

"Super," Timmy said. "Will you look like anyone I want?"

Sati just giggled. I found her answers intriguing, yet I felt far from satisfied. The spell of a moment ago was indeed broken. I wished I could get it back, but the only thing I seemed capable of doing was flapping my tongue. I spoke up again. "But last night you mentioned getting tired of tragedies. What are you going to do to improve our lot?"

"I'm here, am I not?" Sati said.

"Then you do have a purpose in coming?" I asked.

"I'm here to play. If my play should serve to reawaken the silence of your souls, so much the better."

"Sometimes I feel like a bubble that's going down the drain," I remarked, half in jest. "Where does hell fit into all this?"

"There's no drain on my bathtub," Sati said.

"There's no hell?" Timmy asked, pleased.

"No. Why would I make a place to torture people for eternity? People who hold such ideas have a warped opinion of me."

Timmy coughed. "Can we go back to angels? I've always wanted to see one."

Sati lost her smile and regarded him thoughtfully. "You will see many soon, Timothy."

He glanced at me as if to ask if I'd told her about his having AIDS. I shook my head, distressed at her bluntness, and not unduly impressed with her diagnostic abilities. It didn't take an omniscient being to see he was not well.

Timmy forced a chuckle. "That's one of the things I wanted to talk to you about, Sati. Mary was telling me how you fixed up Mrs. Hutchinson's fingers." He hesitated. "I was just wondering if you couldn't help with this cough I've got?"

"Did you go to the doctor?" I asked quickly. From reading, I knew AIDS victims were extremely susceptible to pneumonia.

"Yeah."

"What did he say?" I asked.

"He's got a bad attitude," Timmy said. "He keeps telling me to make out my will."

"Your cough is keeping you from sleeping?" Sati asked.

Timmy nodded, serious for a moment. "It's much worse when I lie down."

Sati reached over and brushed his thinning hair from his forehead. The whites of his eyes were practically yellow. "Come to the meeting tonight," she said. "You'll sleep afterward."

"If you're God, why don't you just cure him?" I asked bluntly. For an instant, I couldn't help it; I was angry with her. Timmy's condition was too serious a matter to be dragged into her fantasy of herself.

Sati's expression remained unaffected. She didn't respond. Timmy was quick to smooth over the awkward moment. "It's cool, Mike. If I get some rest tonight, I'll get over this thing by myself. That's probably how you like to see us do it, right, Sati? God helps those who help themselves, and all that?"

She looked at him. "Usually."

# Chapter 6

The conversation turned to safer topics—politics for one. Timmy got on Sati's case for not being a registered voter and helping in the campaign against the right wing. Her excuse was that she had no last name to put down on the forms.

My anger didn't last, but I had to wonder if I would have to pay for it. For no reason, I began to feel nauseous.

I wondered where Linda and Jenny were. Fred and Nick came to the door next. Fred had with him a bag of groceries and a shapely teenage brunette. This was Lori, the source of all Fred's joy and sorrow. She looked somewhat disappointed when she saw Sati sitting on the couch. Obviously Fred had given Lori a spiel about the cosmic genie he had discovered. Yet this disappointment was nothing compared to her confusion when Timmy suddenly leapt off the couch and started chasing Nick around the living room for a kiss. Nick had once made the serious mistake of commenting in Timmy's presence that he believed the AIDS virus could be communicated by kissing. Since then Timmy had been trying to give it to him. Fortunately or unfortunately, Nick collared Timmy quickly and Timmy started coughing, and that was the end of that. Timmy went back to his place beside Sati.

"He's weird," Lori whispered to Fred, referring to Timmy.

"You just don't know him," Fred said.

"He doesn't try to kiss you, too, does he?" Lori asked, worried.

"Of course not."

Nick took a seat next to me. "Why didn't you go to Phoenix today?" he asked.

"My alarm didn't go off," I said.

Nick smiled big, the scar by his ear twisting. "Got a fireplace in Westwood this morning. It's going to be nice job. I should clear fifteen hundred."

"Wonderful."

Fred introduced Lori to Sati. Hello, how are you? Nice to meet you, God . . . Lori was looking around for the door before she could sit down. I could relate to her restlessness. My stomach was getting worse by the second. I thought doing my laundry might take my mind off it. It was already too late to go looking at rigs.

"You folks will have to excuse me," I said, standing. "I've got washing to take care of."

"Do you need some help, Mr. Winters?" Lori asked.

This wasn't our first meeting. Fred's car had once broken down while he was on a date with Lori. He called me for help. The problem was more serious than a loose battery cable. His electrical system was shorted. I sent him back to my apartment in my car for more tools while I did the best I could with what I had in hand. While he was gone, Lori and I had a *very* friendly talk. I could have been mistaken, but I'd thought several of her remarks suggestive. Naturally, I hadn't told Fred.

"No, I don't need help," I told Lori. "Why don't you stay and get acquainted with Sati?"

"Yeah," Fred said, with a trace of annoyance. "That's why I brought you here."

Before Lori could answer, Sati interrupted. "Go ahead, Lori, help Michael." She grinned at me. "But don't be gone too long."

I would not grant Sati her divine origin, but after I'd been alone with Lori for a few minutes in the downstairs laundry room, I was more than willing to concede that Sati could read body language like no one I had ever met. She *knew* Lori was hot for me. She wanted the two of us alone. No doubt the nearby sexual electricity would increase her infinite bliss.

The advances started innocently enough. Lori

was helping me sort out what was to be bleached and what should be put in cold water. We talked about school and where she wanted to go to college after graduation. Then she suddenly asked about my separation—more specifically, whether I was lonely.

"I work so much, I don't have the time or energy to think about it," I lied.

"But it must be hard when you're used to being with someone."

"It's not too bad."

"But I bet you miss the closeness, don't you?" Lori asked.

"Oh, yeah."

Lori batted her brown eyelashes. "You don't have anything going with that girl, do you?"

"With who?"

"Sati."

"No."

"You're not lovers, or anything?"

"No."

Lori leaned closer, until it was hard to avoid bumping her breasts while working through my clothes. Lori's were not as shapely as Linda's— or for that matter, Sati's—but they were big. It was difficult to look in any one direction and not feel I was looking at them. My stomach began to make deep rumbling sounds that I was sure she would hear and interpret to mean that there was an uncontrollable animal in me waiting to explode.

"I didn't think so," Lori said. "She doesn't seem your type."

I had to smile. "Did you like her?"

Lori wrinkled her nose. "She's nice and all that. She's got great hair. But I've seen better. I don't know why she thinks she's God."

"I see your point."

"To tell you the truth, I think it's pretty immature of Fred to treat her the way he does. He practically worships her."

"She does have a lot of charm."

"Yeah, but I don't see you bowing to her. You're a real mature person, Mr. Winters." She grinned mischievously, and there was a light-year of difference between her grin and Sati's. "You remember that time we were alone together in the car, when we had that fantastic talk?"

"I remember."

"I kept wanting to ask you something. But I was too embarrassed."

"Some things are better left unsaid."

"Mr. Winters, do you think I'm pretty?"

Suddenly, my intestines decided to practice a knot I'd learned in Boy Scouts. The pain was so intense I dropped the clothes I was holding and grabbed my abdomen with both hands. "God," I whispered.

"What's the matter?" Lori cried, hugging my side and squashing her bosom into my ribs. "Is it something I said?"

"I think I'm going to throw up," I breathed, clamping down on my stomach.

"I wasn't trying to come on to you. Please don't tell Fred. There's nothing between us any more, but I don't want him thinking I'd sleep with you behind his back before your divorce is final. Can I get you a drink of water, Mr. Winters?"

"I'll be back in a minute," I moaned. "Stay here and guard my underwear."

Upstairs, the entire gang was jammed in the kitchen making cookies. Timmy was licking the icing knife, grossing everyone out. The thick smell of dough was not what my guts needed. I stumbled toward Sati and touched her arm.

"All right," I said. "Use your powers right now and don't give me any excuses. Why am I sick?"

Sati looked up. "Fred, use your powers right now and tell Michael why he's sick."

"You drank spoiled milk," Fred said.

"Huh?" I said.

"When we made the cookies in my place yesterday, I forgot to put the carton of milk away," Fred explained. "It was a hot day. Sitting out for so long must have ruined it."

"But how did it get in my icebox?" I asked.

"When Sati was helping me deliver the papers this morning, she said she'd be making more cookies this afternoon in your apartment. When we finished the route, I took what stuff I had and jammed it in your refrigerator."

"But why did you put spoiled milk where I would drink it?" I cried.

"I didn't know it was spoiled, Mike," Fred said. "We only discovered it just now." He pulled a carton from my garbage bag. "Here it is if you want to smell it. It stinks."

"No, I don't want to smell it," I shouted, shoving the carton away. Despite my condition, my memory was working extremely well. I remembered how Sati had stared at her glass when I had poured her milk during breakfast. I also remembered that it had tasted funny. "You *knew*," I accused her.

She nodded. "I know everything."

"But why didn't you stop me?"

"I told you I should get the milk. You didn't listen to me. Had I fetched the milk, I would have chosen the carton I used to make the pancakes. That milk was fine."

I bent over with cramps. "I suppose this is all a lesson to teach me to listen to you in the future?" I said bitterly.

"Michael," Sati said. "The only lesson I can think of here is to smell your food before you swallow it."

I tried to straighten. If the pancakes hadn't been so delicious and her company so distracting, I'm sure I would have noticed the smell, never mind the bad taste. "But why didn't you get sick?" I demanded. "I saw you drink the same milk."

Sati leaned against my kitchen counter and patted her belly affectionately. "My tummy works better than yours. I can almost drink poison."

I closed my eyes, taking slow deep breaths.

"What advice does the Almighty have for me now?" I asked.

"Go into the bathroom," Sati said simply. "Stick your finger down your throat, and throw up."

# Chapter 7

The community room in the bank was cozy, with thirty plush chairs and brown carpet deep enough to perform gymnastics on. One wall was solid window and drapes. A striking wallpaper depicting a rusty desert landscape covered the other three. The wallpaper was made up of vivid blown-up photographs, not artistic sketches. I thought it appropriate considering where Sati said she had been born. All of five days ago.

When I arrived for the evening meeting, I was feeling much better. My illness had been as brief as it had been intense. The vomiting had worked wonders. Half the chairs were already occupied and I hesitated to take one for fear there would not be enough. I didn't mind sitting on the floor again. I decided it might even be safer. If I got as settled as I had the previous night, I figured I'd have nothing to fall out of.

There were familiar faces from yesterday. The young couple, and the mother and teen-aged daughter were already present. The four sat with a small group they obviously knew. The only person I saw who could have been considered unusual was a Hare Krishna. He stood in the back. But even he wasn't wearing the traditional saffron gown. It was his haircut that identified him. Plus he had thick black glasses. I don't know why it is, but every Hare Krishna I've ever seen wears thick glasses. Maybe their diet has something to do with it. I understand they eat tons of sugar—the kind of food Sati was so eager to have us consume. Her plate of cherry-topped cookies was sitting up front on a table, beside her sheet-draped chair. As before, there was also a vase of flowers, although this one appeared to have been ordered from the florist. It held a variety of flowers besides roses.

Timmy, Mary, and Nick had arrived before I did. Nick had with him a sketch of Sati he'd been working on most of the afternoon. I assumed he intended to add detail to it during the meeting. As always, his technique was excellent. Mary appeared especially excited about the picture, hugging his arm as she spoke in his ear about his great talent. I felt a stab of envy. They looked so happy together.

David arrived a couple of minutes after me.

His mood was chipper. "Any new developments?" he asked, as we huddled in one corner.

"Sati turned milk to vinegar this afternoon, but other than that, she kept her godhood under her hat."

"What?"

"Nothing," I said. "Timmy and I did have a philosophical discussion with her—the meaning of life and all that. I think it would be safe to say she could hold her own against Plato. It will be interesting to see how she handles strangers' questions."

"She's going to take questions?" David asked.

"She implied this afternoon that she would."

"Great. What's this I hear about Hutchinson's arthritis getting better?"

I waved my hand. "I haven't talked to her myself about it, but even Sati seems to pass it off as unimportant."

David considered for a moment. That was his way. He always thought through the implications of everything before he did anything. That was probably why he was rich. "My sources didn't turn up anything on anyone named Sati," he said finally.

"Who are your sources?" I asked.

"Some people I know."

Secretiveness was another of his characteristics. He disliked telling you where he got his haircut. "I'm not surprised, if all they were using to track her was the name Sati," I said.

David nodded. "We should probably get a

picture of her." He turned toward the chairs. "Let's talk after this is over."

"Fine."

Fred and Lori came in next. Lori wasn't the least bit shy in my presence. Was she so stupid that she didn't see how dangerous it was to make a pass at a boyfriend's buddy? No, she didn't care if Fred found out. She didn't care about Fred. She was a superficial person. Yet I didn't wonder why he was in love with her. I was in no position to think such thoughts.

"Feeling better?" Lori asked sweetly.

"Yes," I said.

Fred snorted. "Lori tells me you almost barfed in her face."

Lori turned red. "I never said that! Fred, tell Mr. Winters I never said that!"

"I did almost barf in your face, Lori," I said, before asking Fred, "Where's Sati? I thought you were bringing her?"

"She wanted to walk."

"Are you serious? The apartment's two miles from here."

Fred shrugged. "She left a while ago. She'll be here soon." He pulled on Lori's hand. "Come on, I want to sit up front."

"I want to sit by the door," Lori said. From listening to Fred, I knew Lori was stubborn, and that he almost always let her have her own way. I was, therefore, pleased with what he said next.

"Suit yourself," he said. He let go of her and

walked to the front. Lori appeared momentarily startled but recovered nicely.

"Where are you sitting, Mr. Winters?" she asked.

"On the floor. Could you excuse me a moment?"

Linda and Jenny had just arrived. Timmy was another of my daughter's favorites. After a quick kiss on my cheek, Jenny hurried to visit with him. Being a liberated woman, her mother wasn't worried about contamination. I ushered Linda out of the room onto the sidewalk.

"Why did you tell Sati you were bringing Jenny over and then never show up?" I asked.

"I changed my mind," Linda said. "I have that right, you know."

"Why didn't you call?"

"I didn't suppose Sati would be sitting around waiting for us."

It was true that Sati had not asked where they were. Yet, to my mind, that didn't make any difference. "You sounded awfully frantic this morning," I said. "What happened?"

"Nothing. The usual. She woke up in the middle of the night crying. She was still upset this morning. But then, as the day went on, she started to cheer up. And I started to ask myself if it was such a good idea for her to be talking to Sati."

"I don't see why not. Sati is a lot nicer than your teachers and psychologists."

"Your hostility toward my teachers is getting

old," Linda said. "Besides, none of them think they're God."

That was a hard point to argue. "Then why did you bring Jenny tonight?" I asked.

Linda frowned. "She told me if I didn't, she would never speak to Dick again."

I laughed.

Back inside, the chairs were filling up quickly. Linda and I were about to plop down on the floor when Mrs. Hutchinson and a stranger entered. I was surprised when she introduced him as the minister of her church. Young and blond, with freckles splashed across his handsome face, he looked more like a surfer off the beach. Yet his dress was conservative, a dark suit and a choker of a red tie. He was carrying a flat black briefcase.

"Mr. Winters, pleased to meet you," he said, crushing my fingers with his powerful handshake. "I understand you've been hosting our guest of honor?"

"She sleeps on my couch," I said.

"Reverend Green has been given a thorough account of what has been going on," Mrs. Hutchinson said.

"How are your hands?" I asked.

She glanced down at them, answered slowly, "They're feeling better today, thank you."

"I'm glad," I said.

Before I could explore the matter further, her eyes focused on Timmy. Pushing her glasses back on her nose, she stalked toward him. "Why aren't you home in bed?" she started. "There's a chill in the night air that can go straight into your chest. Didn't I tell you . . ."

Mrs. Hutchinson disapproved of homosexuality. Fortunately, that didn't keep her from taking care of Timmy. Three months ago he'd caught a flu bug that had been going around, and with an immune system already depressed, his fever had spiked up to 105 degrees. If Mrs. Hutchinson hadn't been regularly checking up on him, he probably would have died of dehydration. He'd been too weak to get out of bed to get a glass of water.

Reverend Green caught my eye. "I've been looking forward to this all day." He glanced around. "Is she here?"

"You'll know when she gets here," I said.

"What's she like?" Reverend Green asked.

"I try to describe her to people and I have the hardest time," I said. "You'll just have to meet her."

"But you seem taken by her," he said.

"Why do you say that?"

"For one, you let her stay at your place," Reverend Green said. "For another, you're telling people about her. I only preach about someone I really believe in. How about you, Mike?"

Somehow the context in which he used my first name did not seem as friendly as, say, when Sati used it. I did not mind. I wasn't going to get into an argument with him over what I believed or disbelieved. *I* didn't know what I believed or disbelieved. If nothing else, Sati had already taught me that one thing.

Still, I was pretty damn sure she wasn't God.

"I like variety in the company I keep," I told the reverend.

He wasn't given a chance to respond. A bright blond head suddenly flashed in the doorway. Every head in the room turned at once.

It was a curious fact that she never looked exactly the same to me. Now her appearance seemed a contradiction in terms. She looked stunning, yet in no way glamorous. Her manner suggested complete authority, and total innocence. As always, her hair hung loose and curly—I doubted she ever combed it. She walked easily, apparently in no hurry, but it wasn't as if she moved slowly. Quite the opposite; she looked very energetic. The green dress she wore was medium length, tied at the waist with a narrow yellow silk sash that had been knotted off center so that the ends hung around her left hip. It must have been one of those Mary had given to her. The colors suited her.

Sati nodded as she passed Reverend Green and me. But she did not pause or speak until she was seated up front. All the chairs were now taken, and a handful of us were still standing. There were approximately forty people present.

"Jennifer," Sati began, "I want you to sit in the back with your father. Sit on his lap. And the rest of you without chairs, make yourselves as comfortable as you can on the floor. You might find it easier on your backs if you lean against a wall."

The chair Jennifer vacated was taken by

Reverend Green. Timmy was now to Green's immediate right.

Why Sati wanted my daughter on my lap was not clear to me, but the weight of her little body on my crossed legs was certainly no burden. Linda settled beside us. The lights were dimmed, and Sati repeated her instructions from the previous night about not minding how we felt during the period of silence. Then we closed our eyes.

This time I experienced no initial restlessness. Almost instantly, I felt my body slow down. It was no mood—my rate of respiration definitely lessened. The other sensations, however, of warmth in the heart and coolness on the forehead, did not occur. Perhaps I was looking too hard for them. But I wasn't disappointed. My overall state of mind was one of steadily increasing peacefulness.

The minutes didn't just vanish as they had in my apartment. For this, I was glad. It gave me more of a chance to savor the rest. God only knew what was bringing it about. A comment Sati had made earlier floated by in my mind:

*"There comes a time for everybody when words and reasons can become such a great weariness."*

After what seemed to be about half an hour, I began to notice an unusual phenomenon. I had started the period with my arms draped loosely around Jenny; then I had forgotten she was even sitting in my lap. Now I began to notice that *something* was pressing against me. What made this so unusual was that this something

101

was not exactly my daughter, and what it was pressing against was not exactly myself. Had I been in an analytical mood, I probably would have gotten all excited and ruined the whole thing. Fortunately, that did not happen. The pressing was actually more of a cuddling. It was extraordinarily pleasant. For the first time in a long time, I felt as though I belonged to someone, and that she belonged to me, and that it would always be that way.

Sati asked us to open our eyes. The silence in the darkened room was so thick it rang. Jenny turned and looked up at me. "I love you, daddy," she whispered.

I pressed my face into her hair. "I love you, too."

"Always?"

"Always and forever."

"I know," she said, nodding to herself. "I know."

Sati welcomed everyone and proceeded to cover the same points as before: she was God; life was meant to be enjoyed; and it was in everybody's best interest to realize their inner being, which was the source of all enjoyment. Her talk lasted maybe five minutes. When she was done she sat waiting, not speaking. Someone raised a hand. It was Reverend Green. Sati nodded slightly. The preacher got to his feet.

"Prove it," he said, and then sat down.

"The silence experienced in my presence is my proof," she said.

"I didn't experience anything," Reverend Green said.

"Silence is subtle," Sati said. "It generally dawns in life without fanfare. Yet it is the most intimate aspect of life. Your inner self is nothing but pure silence. An awareness of silence is the only genuine spiritual experience. Talking in tongues or talking to spirits, healing people or reading another person's mind—these abilities are insignificant compared to the bliss of silence. Be happy with what has happened for you tonight. Contact with me never goes to waste."

Before Reverend Green could argue the point, Sati took a question from a young man who had been to the first talk. He had previously caught my eye. He looked intelligent, like a young math major or something.

"You mentioned talking to spirits," he said. "By that do you mean channeling?"

"Describe this channeling," Sati said.

The young man made a vague gesture. "It's real big in California. All the celebrities visit channels. It's where a person goes into a trance and a disembodied person speaks through them."

Sati nodded. "These sort of things—yes, that is what I meant."

"Is it bad, then?" the young man asked.

Sati shrugged. "Not bad. Not necessarily."

"Is it good, then? I mean, is it valid?"

"I will ask you a question," Sati said. "Say you know a mechanic who lives on the corner. His name is Joe. But he isn't a very good mechanic. You don't have him fix your car when it breaks. Then one day he dies and he begins to speak through a channel. You didn't trust Joe to give your car a tune-up when he was alive. Now are you going to trust him to explain the mysteries of the universe to you just because he's dead?"

The group laughed. The boy smiled and blushed. "Are any of the things that come through channels worthwhile?" he asked.

"Sometimes, yes, you might hear something beneficial."

"How can I tell a good channel from a bad one?" the young man asked.

"It is difficult," Sati said. "Avoid those sources that reflect ego. If a disincarnate spirit tells you that you have been chosen for a divine mission, choose to leave the room."

A well-dressed middle-aged Japanese man raised his hand. He had come with his wife and baby daughter. The baby must have slept through the period of silence. I hadn't heard her.

"Sati, could you speak about free will?" the man asked.

"I am free to speak," she said. "What should I speak?"

"Do we have free will? Or is everything destined?"

Sati stared off into empty space for a long moment. The sense of deep silence in the room was still strong. Yet I could not say that it appeared to emanate from her alone. All of us seemed to be contributing to it in some small way. Sati's answer surprised me.

"Everything is inevitable," she said finally.

"But each day we decide things," the man protested. "For example, I decided to come here tonight. Had I decided to stay home, I would not be here. How do you explain this?"

"Truth is different in different states," she said. "You asked me the question, and I gave you my truth. I am God. But even if you do not accept me as God, if you accept any God, then you must accept him as all knowing. Being all knowing, such a God would have to know you would attend this meeting tonight. Therefore, to believe in God is to believe in destiny."

"Did you know I was going to be here tonight?" the man asked.

"Yes."

"But I almost didn't come."

"In ignorance, the small ego thinks it decides this and that. That is fine. That is how it should be. If in ignorance a man says to himself that everything is inevitable, then he doesn't bother getting out of bed in the morning. What I say about destiny, I say only for your understanding, not as a formula to guide your daily lives. Indeed, in your present state, it is better to believe that you design your own destiny."

"But if it isn't true, why should we believe it?" the man asked.

"You stand in one place. You want to be in another. You get on a bus. You get on the bus knowing you're going to get off. But when you get off, you stand in another place. It is like that. The truth of the goal is not the truth of the path."

"I will have to think about what you have said," the man said.

Sati nodded. "That is good."

The young man raised his hand again. "What does it mean to be enlightened?"

"To be me."

"But how do we get like you?"

"I have not come to show you a particular path. There are many paths. But I will give you direction in choosing one." She paused. "My ways are always simple and natural. They bring immediate fruit, although it may take you some time to realize the value of the fruit. Don't undertake any practice that relies upon talking yourself into a particular state. This cultivates mood-making, nothing more. My silent nature is beyond thought. It cannot be maintained by fanciful moods. This is an important point. Let me repeat it another way. Pure consciousness, Christ consciousness, nirvana, moksha—whatever you want to call it, cannot be gained by thinking about it. Pure being transcends thought. It can only be experienced when the mind slips beyond thought. It cannot be imagined."

Linda stood and raised her hand. "But do we have to travel a path at all? Aren't we always already at the goal? Don't we just have to accept the fact that we can do anything, and do it?"

"That sounds wise. Unfortunately, it is false."

Linda was taken aback. She had obviously expected automatic agreement from Sati. "It sounds to me like you're putting limits on our potential, rather than taking them away," Linda said.

"I am simply being realistic, and reality is different, at present, for you than it is for me." Sati pointed out the window. "That building there is very tall. If you were to go to the top of it, and tell yourself you could do anything, and then jump off the edge, you would quickly discover that your *anything* did not include the ability to fly." The audience chuckled and Sati continued. "You must follow a spiritual discipline. It is through the human nervous system you evolve. You are like light bulbs, endowed with the potential to shine bright. Inside the body you see before you flows a million watts. Yet if an equal amount of energy were to pass through your nervous system, you would go up in a flash of smoke. You must purify your system, and this can only be done through a discipline. It is when the nervous system is perfect that infinity is lived, not before. Practices that do not refine the nervous system, while attempting to expand consciousness, are a waste of time."

Linda was not happy. "But surely you don't believe anyone can tell us how to gain enlightenment? Isn't it something we have to find for ourselves?"

"Certainly it is something you must find for

yourselves, but it is equally true you won't find it unless you learn from someone who already knows where it is. If you want to learn carpentry, you study with a carpenter. If you want to know me, you study with someone who knows me."

"How do we recognize them?" the first young man asked.

"They will remind you of me."

"Wait a second," Linda said. "Are you saying we need a guru?"

"A teacher. Why is that so difficult to accept?"

"Because I grow the most when I decide things for myself," Linda said. "If I just listened to some guru and did what he wanted me to do, I wouldn't get anywhere."

"A true teacher would never tell you what to do," Sati said. "But he would give you the knowledge with which you could decide what would be best for you to do. On the path to me, it is first necessary to come to the understanding that you do not know. This is difficult for most. Everybody likes to think they know. But when you are humble, you can learn a great deal very quickly. Do you understand, Linda?"

"I know what you're saying. I just don't agree with you."

"That is fine, too."

"What about visualization techniques?" Linda asked.

"Yes?" Sati said.

"Do they help us unfold our inner being? I use them a lot in daily life."

"You like them?"

"Yes."

"That is good," Sati said.

Linda showed impatience. "But do you think they have a value?"

"They have a value, certainly. There's value in all these things. But for fathoming the inner being, the value is small. The mind is deep. It is as deep as an ocean. Some small imagination here or there on the surface does not do much. I will give you an example. Say you have cancer. Today, these practices you speak of would have you imagine that you are well. That your body is whole and fit. Now it is you who has created your body. It is you who holds it together. It is you who has made it sick. But all these things you have done from a very deep level of the mind. If on the surface of the mind you imagine that you are healthy, when the deeper part of your mind is saying you're sick, then you only break the connection between the mind and the body further. Lack of mind-body coordination is what leads to sickness in the first place."

Linda was now annoyed. "But studies have shown that people who do visualization exercises get better much quicker. What do you have to say about that?"

"Different studies show different things. If you enjoy these exercises, there is no reason you should stop."

Linda tried a different approach. "What about dreams? I do a lot of work with my dreams. Does this have a value?"

"No. Dreams have different sources. Some come from your daily likes and dislikes. Some arise out of latent impressions in the mind so old you would have trouble imagining. Still others are premonitions. The trouble is, it is impossible to tell what the source is. Also, all dreams, in one form or another, are the release of something. By putting your attention on them, you reemphasize those things the mind is trying to release. It's like sorting through your garbage. It's unnecessary. It's all just garbage. Throw it out."

"So what you're saying essentially is that all my spiritual practices are garbage?" Linda asked. Sati did not respond. She just stared at Linda. It was obviously hard for Linda to take, although I'd always found Sati's stare soothing. "I know for a fact that I feel better when I visualize white light," Linda blurted out. "I feel calmer, less stressed. You're not going to convince me differently."

"I am not trying to convince you of anything," Sati said gently. "But the light is already present inside you. Some small turning of your attention and there it is. There is no need to visualize it. There are other lights besides white. You have seen them?"

Linda stopped. "Yes."

"When?"

SATI

"Before your meeting began. When we were sitting in silence with our eyes closed."

"Our meeting began with silence. Silence follows us all the way through. What lights did you see?"

"White and red and blue."

"You liked them?"

Linda stammered, "Y-yes."

"They are there. They are real. You are full of lights. I see them in you. You are beautiful to me."

Linda suddenly seemed less stressed. "I hope they come back."

Sati shrugged. "It is inevitable."

Linda sat down. The Hare Krishna raised his hand. "Are you saying you are Krishna?" he asked.

"Yes. I even know how to play the flute."

The Hare Krishna smiled and went on, "I agree with much of your philosophy. But your emphasis on having fun in the world contradicts what the scriptures, both Eastern and Western, have to say."

"Where is the scripture that says you mustn't be happy? Show me it and I will tell you that you're not reading scripture at all. However, I am not advocating a hedonist's life-style, unless of course you honestly feel that's what makes you happy. The key word here is 'honestly.' Your intuition is sharper now than when your holy books were written. You are all older and wiser. Your intuition is a truer guide to right action than a list of commandments. Examine

111

what truly makes you happy. Do drugs? How many could honestly answer yes to that? Does cheating other people? Does murdering them? Of course these things do not bring happiness, not even to a serial killer. Do what you feel is best, but don't fret over your mistakes. No one is keeping track of them. Be simple, be natural, and you will come close to being who you really are."

A man who could have been the bank president spoke. "You said we are now older and wiser. Does that mean you believe in reincarnation?"

Sati pulled a flower—it was a carnation—from the vase and played with it. "One carnation should be enough," she said.

The audience laughed again. The gentleman persisted. "But do we grow through many lives?"

"The past is past. If your past goes back ten years, or ten thousand, what difference does it make? You are alive now. This life alone is sufficient to realize me. Don't worry about past lives. Don't worry about future lives. Live now. Enjoy."

The original young man raised his hand. "There are a lot of books nowadays saying this is the dawning of a new age for mankind. Is this true? Should we be optimistic about the future?"

"No," Sati said.

The young man paled. "No? Are things going to get worse? Is the world going to be destroyed?"

"The world will not be destroyed. It has a life insurance policy. That policy is me. But why be optimistic about the future? Why be pessimistic? Why not see things as they are? What will come will come. All your anxieties reside in the past and the future. Your mind feels guilty about something you have done. You worry about what will happen as a result of what you have done. But in the present there are no worries or anxieties. The present is always filled with joy, with love. If you were to live fully in the moment for only a moment, the stress and strain of your entire life would be washed away."

Lori, Fred's girlfriend, raised her hand. "But when people say bad things about you, how can you not worry about it?" she asked.

"What people say about you is their concern," Sati said. "It is not your concern. Don't think too much about life. Live it. Don't think too much about others. If you live your life based on the opinion of others, then you will always be weak. But if you are clear in your conscience, then you will not mind what anybody says about you. It is necessary only that you be naturally helpful to others. And you help others most by being happy. It is very simple."

"But when people say bad things about me I get angry," Lori said. "I can't help it."

"Then get angry. There is nothing wrong with being angry. It is better than pretending you're not. Just don't hit anybody. But keep this thought in mind at the same time. If you accidentally poke yourself in the eye, you do not get angry at your finger. You do not blame your finger. This is because your finger is a part of you. In the same way—and this is not just some high ideal—you are a part of everybody else. Let your anger flow if you must, but understand it is all directed at yourself. Understand it is also the same with your love. All love is directed toward the self."

Lori smiled. "Everything you say is neat."

Sati smiled. "You are neat."

Lori giggled. "You really think so?"

"Yes." Sati looked at Fred. "You haven't raised your hand tonight. Do you have a question?"

"I was wondering if you could talk more about love," Fred said. He glanced back at Lori, who was still glowing from Sati's compliment. "And relationships."

"What can I say about love?" Sati asked. "It is a gift. You cannot make yourself love someone. You either love them or you don't. You cannot make someone else love you."

"You can't?" Fred asked. He sounded disappointed.

"No." Sati played with her carnation. "But you can preserve the love that is already there."

"How?" Fred asked.

"Love is like a seed. Bury it too close to the surface and it dries up from the sun's heat. Bury it too deep and it also dies. Here in the West people keep their love too close to the surface. They see their beloved and right away they say,

'I love you.' Ten times in a single day they will say this, instead of letting that love grow in silence and gain strength. Love can be talked about too much. On the other hand, in the East they have the opposite problem. They don't say anything. They hold it all inside and never let it out. The middle ground is usually best for things, including love. You will remember this, Fred?"

"Yes."

I was steadily gaining more and more respect for Sati's manner of teaching. She did not lecture. Rather she allowed people to draw information from her. Indeed, it was almost as if it was a personal requirement of hers that it be drawn, rather than first offered. Like Linda, I could not say I agreed with everything she said. For example, I found visualization very helpful. When I was driving down the long road, and I was hungry, I often visualized big juicy hamburgers. I was quite adept at it. I could practically taste them. It helped get me to the next stop.

I was never much into daydreaming about lights, though. I wasn't into New Age thought. Sati didn't seem to be either, if Linda's practices were an example of such things. Sati did not appear worried about courting any one group. But she was clever. The continuity of her theme was fascinating. No matter what the topic, she always brought it back to inner silence. Of course, this also made her somewhat repetitious, but each time her angle on the topic was slightly different.

The young man who had already asked so many questions raised his hand again. "Sati, how do we get all this? What do we do? Can't you tell us something that will help us?"

Sati was sympathetic. "What do you want me to tell you?"

The guy spread his hands helplessly. "I don't know!"

Sati nodded. "Ah. A good beginning. Go on."

"I don't know how to go on. I want you to tell me what I should do. You keep talking about gaining inner silence. Does that mean we should meditate?"

"I can't say you *should*. If you don't want to, you shouldn't. But if you are drawn into meditation, that is good. You have tried to meditate already?"

The young man nodded vigorously. "I've tried, but I can't push the thoughts out of my mind."

"Why would you want to try to push the thoughts out of your mind?"

"All the books I've read said your mind has to be empty to meditate. You said the same thing a few minutes ago."

Sati paused. This was a long one. But this time she did not simply stare off into empty space. She took another flower from her vase. She stroked the petals, with her eyes half shut. She seemed to be thinking. No, I should say she appeared to be waiting. Finally, the young man spoke again.

"Could you tell me how to meditate?" he asked.

Sati looked up. "I did not say you should push the thoughts out of your mind. I said pure consciousness can only be experienced when the mind slips beyond thought."

"I don't understand," the young man said.

"You cannot try to free the mind of thoughts. It's not possible. The more you try, the more thoughts you will have."

"Then what should I do?" he asked.

"You are in school?"

"Yes."

"Do you enjoy it?"

"Some of the time."

"Say you have to study for a test," Sati said. "You go out on the lawn at school. You open your book. You focus on the material, and after some time you become absorbed in it. But not far away another student is listening to her radio. One of your favorite songs is being played. Immediately your mind goes to it. But then you realize what you are doing. You have a test coming up. You have to study. You put your mind back on your book. Now maybe forty-five minutes go by. Suddenly you realize that you are not studying. In fact, you haven't been studying for the last ten minutes. You've been listening to the radio again."

The young man nodded. "I know this. My mind is always wandering."

"The mind does not just wander. It wanders in a direction. The music is charming. The book is boring. When you were not thinking about it, your mind automatically went to the music. The reason for this is what I have been saying all along. It is the nature of the mind to seek out greater happiness. It does so automatically. It is the same for everyone. There are no exceptions. The purpose of life is the expansion of happiness. Now let us take this understanding and apply it to a method of going within. Have not all wise men throughout time spoken of the inner self as perfectly silent, the source of perfect joy?

"Yes," the young man said.

"They said this because it is true," Sati went on. "But being perfectly silent it cannot be reached by someone who is trying to reach it. When you try, you create more activity in the mind, more thoughts. That takes you farther away from your goal. It is a paradox."

"Is there nothing you can do?" the young man asked.

"There is the nature of the mind. If the mind could be turned properly inward—just slightly— then it would begin to settle. Why? Because the greatest happiness resides inside. There would be no effort. There would be no doing. Nature would carry out the whole process. Meditation is a technique whereby you allow the mind to do what it's always wanted to do. It is nothing more. It is always very simple, natural, and easy. With this understanding in mind, you will learn how to meditate correctly. Have no worry about this."

The young man was reassured. "Thank you."

Sati responded with a slight nod.

The bank president raised his hand again. "Sati, is meditation the only way to God?" he asked.

"It is not that way," she said. "Even though I have spoken of a path, there is no path as such to God. Linda was right there. This is the trouble with words. Answers given in words create more questions, even while they are being spoken. Only in silence is there perfect communication. One only finds God by grace, and grace alone. Grace is like the sweet rain that falls from the sky. You are like cups. You have to catch this grace as it falls. Meditation allows you to keep your cup turned upward so that when the rain comes, you are ready to receive it."

"Is there no other way?" the man asked.

"There is service," Sati said. "Service to others with the understanding that one is serving oneself also allows grace to enter."

The man was embarrassed. "This is hard for me. When I saw you yesterday, I thought you were the most extraordinary person I had ever met, even though I did not believe you were God. And now tonight, after sitting in silence with you, I am even more confused. It is so beautiful just to be here in your company. And I don't know why!"

"What is so hard about this?" Sati asked.

"Are you really God?"

"Yes."

The man shook his head. "I'm a Christian. Christ is my master."

"Yes."

"If I were to accept that you are God, could I accept you as my master along with Christ?"

"No," Sati said without hesitation. A distinct discomfort went through the room. I noticed Reverend Green shaking his head. Mrs. Hutchinson stared at the floor. Sati continued. "You cannot have two masters."

"Then I would have to reject Christ to follow your teaching?" the man asked, clearly upset.

"No," Sati said, and she smiled. "We are not talking about rejecting anything, much less Christ. But to follow his teaching, and mine—if that is what you want to call what I say—then you will have to understand that it is the same teacher that has come to you in two different bodies. I am Christ. I am the son of God. I am also the mother of God. I am Sati. There is nothing but me."

The man looked relieved. "Being a Christian, I feel I have to be born again to know God. Could you speak on what it means to be born again?"

"This is a beautiful question. Usually what is said in the scriptures is in the form of metaphor. Things cannot be taken too literally or the meaning will be lost. Nevertheless, in this case the expression is clear. To be born again means one must die." Sati gestured with her hands, with her palms open and slowly descending as she spoke. "As the mind settles deep into that inner silence, the body slows down. This is one of the criteria for true spiritual experience. The breathing slows down, and eventually it stops. You know those wonderful mystical experiences that people report when they brush close to death? They come as a result of the cessation of breath. When the breath stops, the mind is set free. One is only born again when one dies. Deep meditation is like death, even though one comes out of it feeling much more alive. A true Christian is he who experiences the depths of his inner being."

"Could you speak about the value of prayer?" the man asked.

"Prayer has great power if the mind is settled. A prayer from the heart is always heard. But don't pray for things. You might get them, and then you probably won't want them. I know what you need. Let me decide what to give you. But if you wish, if someone you know is ill, you may pray for them. I will heed that prayer. Yet know that the highest form of prayer is one that is offered in love, just in love—a prayer that asks for nothing, that trusts in the perfect order of things. I tell you, without any doubt, everything is inevitable. Don't fret in prayer about what is to be, or what should have been. Prayers should be fun, joyful. But if you don't love me, if you're not happy with me, then remain silent and listen to me. For everybody, prayer should end in silence, in meditation."

"Is there a value in traditional prayers?" the man asked. "For example, the Lord's Prayer? Or should we pray as we feel to pray?"

"There is great value in tradition. All the religions of the world have their different prayers. I listen to them all. I wrote them all. Many years of repetition have endowed these prayers with power. Yet if you choose to make up a prayer, I will also listen to that. Remember my names when you pray, my true names. Sati is but one of them. There are many others. No one religion has a lock on the truth. Each knows bits of the truth. But only those bits that lead one to a realization of the inner being have value."

"Thank you," the man said.

"Very sincere questions," Sati said. "It is good."

A bearded fellow in a wheelchair near the wall raised his hand next. He wore an army fatigue jacket and I would have laid odds he had served in Vietnam and seen action. Having just missed the war, I always felt guilty whenever I came face to face with guys like him. What I'd gone through in life always seemed insignificant compared to that.

"If I understand you correctly," the guy said, "you're telling us to look after number one?"

"Who else is there?" Sati asked.

"That sounds selfish to me. Shouldn't we place the needs of our brothers before our needs?"

"You will not become selfish seeking me. I am

in all people. Move a step closer to me and you move ten steps closer to the rest of humanity."

"I'm afraid that's a bit too abstract for me to swallow."

"Only the strong can help the weak. If you go to console a friend in the hospital, and while you're there you catch his disease and start coughing in his face, how have you helped him? A man—or a woman; I speak of both, of course—who finds me is never ill. He is always strong. Nothing can harm him. He does the greatest service to humanity. By his mere presence, he brings life and joy to all. Such men and women are more important to the world than any number of those who labor to help their fellow man. Don't misunderstand me, those who serve are performing good works, especially if their service brings them personal satisfaction. But if their labors don't, if they sacrifice and suffer in the name of God, then they would be better off going into another line of work. A do-gooder who suffers does no good at all."

The crippled man nodded. "It's interesting what you say."

Sati regarded him closely. "You wanted to ask another question?"

He lowered his head shyly. "It's not actually a question. When you were talking about how life is meant to be enjoyed, I couldn't help wondering where I went wrong."

"You refer to your spinal injury?" Sati asked.

"Yeah, among other things."

"You have memories you wish you could forget?"

He glanced up. "Yeah, sure do."

"When you were sitting a few minutes ago with your eyes closed, how did you feel?"

He started to speak, stopped, thought for a moment, then sighed. "I felt great."

"Like you were flying?"

He was surprised. "Yeah."

"It is true you evolve through the body, but no injury or sickness, no matter how severe, can prevent you from finding me if your search is sincere." She smiled. "Why worry about walking when you can fly?"

He smiled. "I'll try to remember that."

"I'll remember you."

He lowered his head again. "Thanks. The name's Kurt."

"I know your name."

Reverend Green stood again. I had been waiting for him to do so. His expression was not quite as pleasant as when he had entered. "Miss, may I speak?" he said.

"Yes."

He cleared his throat. "First I would like to congratulate you on your style of presentation. You have the remarkable talent of satisfying people's questions without saying anything. But—"

"Thank you," she interrupted. "I agree completely with you that words are unsatisfactory. That is why I told you silence is my only proof."

"But," he continued with a note of impatience, "not all of us have such a luxury. Like this gentleman here, I am a Christian. I am also a minister, and as such, I must back up everything I say with the Holy Bible." He paused. "Do you accept the Bible as true?"

Sati reached for more flowers to play with. "Parts of it are nice."

"Which parts do you like?"

"The parts that talk about me," she said.

The minister allowed a trace of a smile. "Offhand, I don't recall your name mentioned once in either the Old or the New Testament."

"Wherever the joy of the Lord is discussed, there I am."

"So you're a happy God?"

"Yes."

"And you're the Second Coming of Christ?"

"If you like."

"Are you or aren't you?"

She grinned. "I'm Sati. I'm just a girl."

"But you say you're God."

"We're all God." Sati found a red rose she liked and began to caress it along with her other flowers. "The only difference between you and me is that I know I am God."

Reverend Green checked around the room to make sure he had everyone's attention. "Do you believe Christ was like you, that he knew he was God?" he asked.

"Yes."

"Excellent. Now, being omniscient, you must also know that Christ said in the Gospel of John—chapter five, verse sixteen—'I am the way, the truth and the light. No one comes to the Father except through me.' Would you agree that he said this?"

"Yes," Sati said.

"Then you would also have to agree that his words make you a liar?"

"Not at all. The statement is entirely impersonal. Christ is not speaking of the individual personality he took on as Jesus. He is referring to his inner reality, which is the same infinity Krishna and I experience. Krishna said he was the only God. I say I am the only God. None of us is lying. We are all the same being."

The reverend tried another approach. "Do you believe that Christ died on the cross for our sins?"

"You are all responsible for yourselves. That is how it must be if you are to learn from life. Christ wouldn't have been so foolish as to try to take away important lessons from anybody."

"That's not what the Bible says."

"If you are trying to get me to agree with everything the Bible says, we will be here all night and the cookies I baked this afternoon will go to waste. But your difficulty is not with the Bible. From the right perspective, it can be of great value. It is a beautiful book. I wrote parts of it. No, your difficulty is a lack of awareness of your inner being. You see difference everywhere. You even go so far as to take God out of man and put him up in heaven." Sati smiled, her eyes lighting up the room. "When she's really sitting right here in front of you."

126

He wasn't amused. "What if I told you I thought you were deluded? That you were a mouthpiece for the devil?"

"I wouldn't hold it against you. There is no devil as you understand him. If you consider for a moment with an open mind, you will see that to accept a devil who operates outside the will of God is to accept a God who isn't omnipotent. Obviously, this can't be. Nothing happens except through the will of God. Even what you would call evil has its place in God's design."

Reverend Green's voice was cold. "I'm sure you would know that better than most."

"That is correct. I am as evil as I am good. I am all things, and yet, I am beyond all things. There is nothing higher than me. I am Sati."

I had been enjoying the show so far, but now I began to feel anxious. I did not know why. Mr. Green was a minister Mrs. Hutchinson had known for years. He was obviously getting irritated, but surely, I thought, he wouldn't get violent. He reached for his black briefcase.

"You are great at twisting things," he said. "But I think it's time to put you to the test. Mrs. Hutchinson informs me you told her earlier today that Christ never suffered. You said his death and resurrection were shams."

"His death and resurrection were facts. I never said they were shams, nor did Carol tell you I did. But Christ never suffered. How could he suffer? Only the weak suffer. And he was far stronger than you can imagine."

Reverend Green snapped open his briefcase. "And I suppose you never suffer either?"

Sati smiled. "Nail me on a cross and I'll still be smiling."

"I'm glad you put it that way," the minister said softly, removing a heavy hammer and a long nail from his briefcase. An unhappy stir shook the room. Linda's head twisted toward me and I quickly removed Jenny from my lap and stood. Nick set aside the drawing of Sati he had been working on, freeing his hands in case things got nasty. He had one eye on the minister and one eye on me. If I gave the sign, he would pick Green up and toss him out on the pavement. Unaware of this, Reverend Green enjoyed the commotion he'd started. He gave everyone a good look at the sharpness of the nail. Faces darkened. Sati continued to play with her flowers.

"Is there a problem here?" Reverend Green asked. "Doesn't anyone besides me want a demonstration?"

"I, for one, do not need a demonstration," the bank president said, angry.

"Bill, please," Mrs. Hutchinson said, trying unsuccessfully to get his attention.

"Put that away," I said sharply.

Reverend Green nodded. "I assure you, I have no wish to harm this young lady. But at the same time, I cannot sit idly by while she desecrates the Bible."

"Why not?" Timmy asked.

The reverend spoke firmly. "Because I am a soldier in the war against Satan."

"Sorry, I didn't know," Timmy said.

"There'll be no demonstrations," I said. "This is a friendly get-together. Put your tools away now or leave."

I had the group on my side, that was clear, but the guy didn't care. He turned to Sati. "What do you say, girl? Want to accept the challenge and show these people that you're more than talk?"

Sati put down her flowers. "What is the challenge, sir?"

He cleared his throat. "You set the conditions with your own remark. I'll hammer this nail through your hand and you'll keep smiling."

People gasped. Without hesitating, Sati rested her hand on top of the table that held the vase of flowers. "Very well," she said. "If you honestly feel it will make you happy."

The room buzzed with anxious chatter. Everyone sounded opposed to the idea. I moved toward the front. Nick also got to his feet. "You're a weird dude," I said, placing myself between him and Sati. "Get the hell out of here."

"Bill, I think that would be best," Mrs. Hutchinson said, tugging on his shirt. He brushed her off and stepped in my direction, the nail and hammer in his hand.

"This is between the young lady and me," he said. "If she wants to play God, she's going to have to pay the price."

Nick was asking me with his eyes if he wanted me to stop it his way. I shook my head, putting my hand on the minister's arm. "This is your last chance, buddy," I said. "Leave, or we'll make you leave."

He laughed. "Are you a bodyguard or what? Does your God need them? Jesus didn't need any. He was the genuine article." His voice hardened. "I'll leave the second she admits to being a phony."

"Hey, let's just eat the cookies and call it a night," Timmy said.

Mrs. Hutchinson came up behind her minister. "Bill, I don't like this. It's not proper."

He ignored her, looking past me at Sati. "You're not talking, girl," he said. "Are you afraid?"

"Michael, let the soldier pass," Sati said.

I turned toward her. "Are you crazy?"

"You have been wondering that since you picked me up. No, I am not crazy. Let him do what he wants."

"No way," I told her. "He says he's going to pound a hole in your hand and he'll do it. I've seen these kinds of guys before."

"Trust me," Sati said. "Everything will be all right."

I looked in Sati's eyes. If I was looking for a sign of fear, I looked in vain. She was actually enjoying herself. But it was at the expense of others. At the rear of the room, my daughter was cringing in her mother's arms. People were

130

biting their nails. Mrs. Hutchinson was trembling.

"Trust me," Sati repeated.

I let go of the minister's arm, saying, "Nick, get rid of this creep."

Nick strode forward. Mr. Green took one look at him, knife scar and all, and backed up fast. Some might have thought it funny that he backed behind Sati for protection.

"If you cooperate, reverend," Nick said, "you'll be able to get out of bed tomorrow morning."

"I'm not leaving till I've made my point," he swore.

Nick sighed and glanced at me. The preacher was apparently willing to take it as well as dish it out. The situation was almost comical. "He'll break you in two," I warned.

"Nick, let him do what he wants," Sati said.

"I'm afraid I can't do that," Nick said, cracking his knuckles.

Sati closed her eyes for a second, then reopened them. In that brief moment, her face had changed. Suddenly, it was stern. "You'll do as I say," she said.

Nick dropped his arms to his sides. I found I had taken a step away from her. The chatter in the room ceased. I could almost hear my heartbeat. Sati turned behind her.

"They will not harm you, William," she said to the minister.

"Sati," I began.

"Be silent, Michael." She raised her hand— the one she was offering to sacrifice—to stop others from protesting. But her tone returned to normal, softening. "Shh, be quiet, all of you. Nothing can hurt me."

Reverend Green slowly emerged from his hiding place, coming around Sati on her right. Once again she laid her right hand on the table beside the vase of flowers. It occurred to me then—it was really an extraneous thought— that I didn't know if she was right-handed or left-handed. She seemed to use both equally well.

"I've got to say one thing for you, girl," Reverend Green said. "You know how to put on a show."

Sati nodded.

The minister weighed the hammer in his hand. "Are you sure you want to go through with this?" he asked.

"Are you?" she asked.

He fidgeted. "You're nothing."

"Am I?"

He reached out and centered the nail in her palm. I could not believe I was allowing it to happen. I had to ask myself if *I* was the one who wanted a demonstration. But that could not be possible, I thought. There was nothing I wanted from Sati. There was nothing she had to prove to me. She wasn't God. There almost certainly wasn't one.

A faint whimpering sound caught my attention. It was Lori, of all people, with tears streaming over her cheeks.

"You're not smiling," Reverend Green said.

Sati smiled warmly for him. The minister quickly removed the nail from her palm. He was getting exasperated. He wasn't quite the psycho he appeared, I realized. He must have listened to Mrs. Hutchinson half the day on the phone and gotten himself all worked up about all the ways he would set Sati straight. He had probably brought the nail and hammer thinking she would back down. Yet here she was, goading him to go through with it.

I realized she could very well *force* him to do it.

"I could damage your nerves," he said.

"You could," Sati said.

"But nerves don't heal. I don't think you know what you're doing."

"It is you who are doing it."

"Look, even the Lord cried out when the Romans tortured him. What makes you think you are greater than he?"

Sati spoke softly. "*I* never cried out."

Reverend Green stuck his nail back in her hand. "Your insolence will be the death of you." He raised the hammer. "I'm going to do it."

Sati nodded, watching him.

"You'll bleed just like anyone else. You're no better."

"Do it."

He stood frozen forever. Then he let the hammer fall. It hit the head of the nail squarely. The room choked on the sound of the contact. Sati kept right on smiling.

She wasn't bleeding. Reverend Green had

lost his nerve. At the last instant, he'd moved the nail aside. It was now stuck in the table, between her fingers.

"You missed," Sati said, a note of irony in her voice.

My paralysis left me. Striding forward, I snatched the hammer from Reverend Green's hand and shoved him back. It was Sati, however, whom I glared at. "You're wearing on my bliss," I said.

She laughed. "Does this mean you're not going to give William another whack at me?"

Reverend Green was standing as if he were in shock. He swallowed thickly. "I didn't want to hurt you," he murmured.

"Could have fooled me," Timmy said.

"You haven't hurt me," Sati reassured Reverend Green, flexing her hand for all to see.

Green was still a stubborn minister. "This proves nothing."

Sati nodded. "You love your God. You are a fine person. But you need to learn to love other people's God, too. And you will." She bid him come closer. She reached for her plate of goodies. "Have a cookie."

Reverend Green glanced at the people in the audience—who weren't by any stretch of the imagination fans of his—and decided it was no time for dessert. "I'd better go . . . Sati," he stammered, moving to leave.

She grabbed his hand and squeezed it gently. "You said my name, William. That is good. That is a beginning."

He gave her a last look, his cocky expression having given way to confusion, and then left.

Mrs. Hutchinson did not go after him. Glancing at Sati's hands, then at her own, she returned to her seat and sat down.

Sati finished the lecture with a minute of silence. It was quite potent. It erased the tension from the room.

"We'll meet again tomorrow night," she told the audience when they opened their eyes. "Same time, same place. Feel free to bring your family and friends. Thank you for coming." She stood and spoke to me. "I'll be walking back to your apartment now."

I had grabbed a quick seat at her feet for the minute of silence. "Can't I give you a ride?" I asked, looking up.

"I like to walk."

"You know, you scared me for a moment there."

"Not as much as I scared him." She patted me on the top of the head. "I'll talk to you before you go to bed."

# Chapter 8

I t was an hour before the room
cleared. People apparently like to so-
cialize after being zapped. I talked
to a few of them. The majority felt they had
definitely experienced something while sitting
with their eyes closed. Most described it as a
feeling of peacefulness. *Everyone* agreed Sati
had nerves of steel.

In the end, four of us were left: David, Timmy,
Nick, and I. Fred had wanted to talk with me
alone, but he'd had to leave with Lori. The
episode with the nail had upset her greatly.

"We have to talk," I said when the last guest
was gone. We were arranged in a rough circle,
finishing the last of Sati's cookies. Tiny white
cups were scattered atop a few of the chairs. A

couple of people from the previous night had brought juice. The cleanup would only take a few minutes. There was no hurry. The bank president had told me to put the room key through the front door mail slot when we were done.

"I'm ready to sign up," Timmy said with a laugh. "A religion that doesn't believe in suffering is what I've been waiting for."

"But Sati said she didn't want to start a religion," I said.

"Yeah, and she told me Christ didn't want to, either," Timmy said. "It's up to us." He punched Nick on the shoulder. "You can write the Gospel According to St. Nick."

Nick smiled grimly. "What do you want to talk about, Mike?"

"Let me start with a stupid question," I said. "Everyone who thinks she's God, raise your hand." No one raised his hand. "Now what?"

David leaned forward. "Is it possible that she could be telling us the truth, but that we are misunderstanding her?"

"Seems to me she's either the top boss or she's not," Nick said.

"Then you think she's lying?" I asked.

Nick shook his head. "I don't want to say that, especially after tonight."

"That's how I feel," Timmy said. "I like her. She's wonderful. Maybe she isn't really God, but an angel. She said they've got great senses of humor."

"Please, let's not get started on angels again,"

I said. "Dave, what did you mean with your question?"

Our landlord was confused, and he didn't like it. "You were the philosophy major," he said. "Is there any middle ground here?"

I took a moment to collect my thoughts. "There are a number of traditions in the world that deal with the state of enlightenment. The Buddhists and the Hindus are the obvious ones, but there's also the Sufis and the Jains. Not to mention many of the modern-day groups. They teach philosophies similar to Sati's: that everything is pure being, and nothing else. That there is only one being, and that we are all ultimately it. In most of these traditions, when a man gains full enlightenment, he is said to be identical to the supreme being. Sati herself has indicated that when we really know her, we become her."

"Then you're saying Sati could simply be an enlightened person?" David asked.

"I'll go for that," Nick put in. "Those yogis in India are supposed to have all kinds of unusual powers. I once saw a photograph of one of those guys floating in the air."

Timmy seconded the idea. "She has yogic characteristics. Notice the way she sat on the couch this afternoon. She was in the half lotus. Also, she sits so still, like she's meditating even when she's talking to us. And, of course, she gives off that great feeling."

"There are two problems with this idea," I said. "First, we can't say she is *simply* an enlightened person, not the way she defines enlightenment. If she is, then she is all-knowing and all-powerful. There would be no difference between her and God. We would be back where we started from. Second, she's not saying she's your typical master or yogi. She says her body did not come into existence until a few days ago."

"Does she have a belly button?" David asked. Nick and Timmy broke up. David went on, "I'm serious. Does she?"

Timmy smiled. "I'm an expert on bodily orifices. She's got one."

"How do you know?" I asked.

"I tickled her this afternoon," Timmy said.

"Is she ticklish?" Nick asked.

"Extremely," Timmy said.

"Let's not get sidetracked," David said.

"Does a belly button mean anything?" Nick asked. "When she formed her body, she could have added a belly button."

"If she didn't have one," I said, "it would be a hell of a lot easier to believe her story." I took a bite of a cookie. All the sugar was giving me a rush, and it didn't appear to matter that God had baked them. "Let's look at the facts. What has she done that demonstrates supernatural abilities? We've already covered her vibes. What else have we got?"

"She's not afraid of anything," Nick said.

"She's sharp, incredibly sharp," Timmy said.

I nodded. "She can handle a tractor and

trailer. Plus she doesn't seem to need much sleep."

"Have you seen her sleep at all?" David asked.

"I've seen her sit perfectly still in my truck for several hours with her eyes closed," I said.

"Have you ever seen her lie down and sleep?" David asked.

"No, but I haven't spied on her in the middle of the night."

"Check on her tonight," David said.

"I'll try," I said.

David was unhappy. "We're not getting anywhere. Except for her vibes, nothing we're listing is that out of the ordinary."

"Yeah," Timmy said. "Imagine how far the apostles would have got telling people what a groove it was sitting with Jesus. They had his miracles to fall back on. We need one."

Nick shrugged. "What about Mrs. Hutchinson's hands?"

"Too vague," I said, glancing at Timmy. "Hey, how come you're not coughing?"

"I . . ." he began, before a beatific grin spread across his bony face. "I don't know. Wow, that's right. I haven't coughed since her period of silence."

Everyone sat up. "But are your lungs clear?" I asked. "Take a deep breath."

Timmy took a deep breath, and started coughing. We all sat back in our chairs. "But I do feel better," Timmy said.

"How do you feel, Mike?" Nick asked.

"You mean, my stomach? It's almost back to normal."

Nick clasped his big hands together. "But you were pretty sick. And you say you're sure Sati drank the same spoiled milk that you did."

"What's this?" David asked.

I explained what had happened, finishing with the remark, "It doesn't prove anything. She herself said she just has a strong stomach."

"But she also said she could drink poison," Timmy said.

"She said that?" David asked quickly.

"Yeah," Timmy said.

David was impressed. "When it's come to day-to-day things, has she always been right?"

"She is extraordinarily perceptive," I said. "When I picked her up, we stopped at a diner. There's a waitress who works there who lost her husband to cancer years ago. This woman thinks about him constantly. She's never remarried. Sati noticed her wedding ring and said, I quote, 'The ring is very nice. You wear it well.'"

"So?" David said.

"I've known Penny a long time," I said. "I've never told her that, but it's something I've often thought. Sati seemed to grasp Penny's background immediately." I shrugged. "Then again, she might have simply meant that the ring looked nice on Penny's finger."

"Anything else?" David asked.

"Yes," I said. "She predicted yesterday morning that no one would complain to the *Times* about the flyers she stuck in Fred's papers. So far, according to Fred, no one has. She often refers to things that end up happening. She told my daughter she would see her at yesterday's meeting. It looked like a remote possibility at the time, but Jenny ended up coming. She told me I would be here tonight, and here I am."

"But she turned off your alarm, didn't she?" Timmy asked, yawning loudly. "She arranged for you to be here."

"That's true," I said.

Our profound discussion faltered. The four of us sat eating cookies and wishing they would magically multiply into thousands, as fish and loaves of bread were reputed to do on such occasions. Timmy started to cough again.

"Hey, man, you should be in bed," Nick said. "Let me take you home."

Timmy nodded. "I should go, yeah. But it's been nice to get out like this, and be around people."

The innocent remark made it hard for me to swallow the bite of cookie I had in my mouth. Timmy's parents had disowned him five years earlier when he had told them he was gay. They didn't even know he was dying. He had no brothers or sisters. He had no money. It was sad, all he had was us.

"Need anything?" David asked. He could be a tight bastard, but with Timmy he had always been generous. Before his illness, Timmy had been an electrician. Since being put on perma-nent disability, he had been doing electri-

143

cal maintenance on David's properties in exchange for an apartment. Since this maintenance amounted to no more than a few hours' labor a week, David was essentially giving him the apartment free. Indeed, for the last couple of months, Timmy had been too sick to work at all.

"I'm fine, thank you," Timmy said.

"Don't play the martyr with me," David said. "If you need a few bucks, tell me."

Timmy nodded. "OK, I would like some money. But not for myself. I'd like to buy Sati a present."

"What can you buy a girl who has everything?" I asked.

"It's a secret," Timmy said.

David took out his wallet. "Will a hundred be enough?"

"I won't need that much," Timmy said.

David gave him a hundred, anyway. "Nick, take this guy home. And could you leave that sketch of Sati? I'd like to look at it."

Nick stood and handed David his drawing pad. The picture was remarkable. Nick had caught Sati's joyful nature without having to resort to putting a big smile on her face. "I'm sort of proud of it," Nick said.

"Who knows?" David said, hardly glancing at it. "Maybe someday it will be worth a fortune."

"It won't be for sale," Nick said. Then he scratched his head and laughed.

"What's so funny?" I asked.

"It's nothing," Nick said. "It has nothing to do with Sati."

"Tell us," Timmy said.

Nick was embarrassed. "It just struck me tonight that Mary's going to have *my* kid. It's weird, it never really hit me before." He helped Timmy up. "I should get home to her."

Timmy feigned weakness and leaned against Nick's body. "My heart," he gasped. "You'll have to carry me up the stairs."

"I can carry you," Nick said. "Just don't try to kiss me."

Timmy beamed. "She must be God. All my dreams are coming true."

When they were gone, I asked David, "What do you want the drawing for? A photograph would be better for tracing her."

David nodded. "Try to get one. Are you making a run to Phoenix tomorrow?"

"Yes."

"Do you have a Polaroid?"

"No."

"Ordinary film usually takes overnight to develop. Nick's sketch might be the only picture you'll have to take with you."

"You want me to show her face to people who live near where I picked her up?" I asked.

"If you have the time. I know it's a long shot. For all we know, she could have hitchhiked from the other side of the country."

"It may not be the long shot you imagine. When I was in that diner with Sati, this guy kept staring at her as if he knew her. He works down the road in Catson in a factory. I don't remember his name, but Penny—the waitress I mentioned—will tell me what it is. In fact, Penny herself thought Sati looked familiar."

"It's a lead. We've got to find out where she came from before we . . ." David didn't finish.

"Before we what?" I asked.

He chuckled, shaking his head. "If she impressed me yesterday, she blew my socks off tonight. Did you see how calmly she sat there while that idiot threatened her with that nail? I say it again, she's got magic, God or no God. We've got to get her on TV." He glanced at the chair where she had been sitting. "Do you like having her at your place?"

"She keeps things lively."

"Not too lively, I hope."

"What do you mean by that?" I asked.

He waved his hand. "Nothing, don't get shook. I was just thinking, it doesn't look good that she's living with a guy. Not for someone in her position. People will talk."

"Sati doesn't seem to care what people talk about."

"That's what she's got us for, to look after her better interests."

"Dave, can I ask you a blunt question? Why are you, on the one hand, trying to prove she's a phony, and on the other hand, trying to launch her as a celebrity?"

"Before you launch a ship, Mike, it's smart to check first and see what could sink her."

# Chapter 9

When I came through my apartment door, Sati was sitting cross-legged on the couch in an orange robe Mary had lent her. The lighting was down low. Her hair hung close to her cheeks, partly hiding her face.

"I brought these back," I said. I had the vase of flowers and the plate of cookies in my hand.

Sati nodded.

"How was your walk?" I asked.

"Fine," she replied softly.

"Your talk tonight was interesting."

She nodded.

"Is something wrong?"

She slowly turned toward me. "No. Sit here beside me."

I set down the flowers and plate on the coffee table and joined her on the couch. She had showered; her hair was wet.

"You're lucky you escaped with your hand in one piece," I said.

"There was never a chance of him hurting me."

"You can read people that well?"

Her mood was solemn. "Yes."

"I don't know," I said. "You've got to be careful with guys like that. They're fanatics, totally unpredictable."

"You are also a fanatic. You're in love with your image of Linda. Mr. Green is in love with his image of Jesus. Both of your images have little to do with reality. Both of you are making yourselves miserable."

"That's not fair, comparing me to him. You don't see me hammering nails in people."

"You prefer to hammer them through your own hands."

"And what's that supposed to mean?" I asked.

"You know."

"You keep telling me . . ." I began, catching myself when I heard the anger entering my voice. I hate to get angry. I always get mad at myself when I do. Yet it seemed nowadays I only had to hear my wife's name and I would lose my cool. For that reason, I decided I really didn't want Sati to elaborate on her remark. Nick must have explained the details of the divorce to Sati. I'd have to tell him to mind his own business. "Never mind," I muttered.

Sati nodded. Her robe was wrapped loosely about her slender frame. For all I could tell, she wasn't wearing anything underneath.

"I was surprised the minister didn't have a change of heart after losing his challenge," I said.

"He changed."

"Do you think he's going to come see you again?"

"No."

"What if he had driven the nail through your hand? It would have to have hurt you."

She turned her big eyes on me. "You see the body of a young woman in front of you. This body can suffer. But I am more than the body. I never suffer."

"But you are affected by stuff? At least in a superficial way?"

"No."

"Sati, I asked you this yesterday—do you sleep?"

"Sleep does not affect me. I am beyond waking, dreaming, and sleeping. That is why I do not ask for your belief in me. If you believe I am God, that belief will vanish when you sleep. If you believe Christ is God, that belief will vanish when you sleep. When you sleep, you are all atheists. Can't you see how fragile belief in God is, that something so simple as sleep can wipe it out? But when I am truly found, sleep never steals me away. When I am within a man or a woman, I am there to stay."

"Sounds neat," I muttered, not minding that

she hadn't really answered my question. Her point of view was simple, yet the more I thought about it, the more profound it seemed. To her, understanding reality didn't depend upon adopting a certain attitude. She was strictly into experiencing reality. "Hey, I wanted to ask about what happened tonight during your period of silence. I felt . . ."

"You talked to your daughter after the meeting?" she interrupted. Like many of her questions, it could have been a statement.

"Yes. To Linda and Jenny both. Linda finally broke down and admitted you were one amazing creature, whoever you are. But that minister scared Jenny. I hope she doesn't have another bad night because of it."

"Her bad nights were because she was afraid she would lose you. That fear is gone."

"Really? That's what I wanted to talk to you about. When I was sitting there, I felt . . ."

"Shh. Too many words, Michael, about things better left inside."

"All right." I settled back on the couch. Her tone had not lightened. This serious Sati was in some ways frightening, and in other ways even more beautiful. Her long lashes brushed the strands of damp hair clinging to the side of her face. The collar of her robe was loose; the top of her left breast was visible. I was by no means feeling hot for her, but all of a sudden I felt a real strong desire to hug her. Of course, I kept my hands to myself. "Can I take your picture?" I asked.

"No."

"You'll have to have a picture taken some time. If your meetings continue to grow, like it or not, you're going to be in the papers."

"Word of mouth alone is sufficient to spread the news of my coming."

"This is L.A. Get a cult following here and they'll put you on TV for sure."

"I will never be on TV."

"That's not what David thinks."

Sati did not answer. She just looked at me strangely.

# Chapter 10

The wind was dry and dusty as I stepped from my truck into the afternoon sun and walked toward Pete's diner. A tumbleweed bounced by. I looked at the brown desert and thought of ghost towns and skeletons in the closet, and ships I might not want to sink. Still, I went inside the diner anyway, Nick's sketch clutched close to my heart. I asked to speak to Penny.

She wasn't there, which was no major surprise. I was on my way to Phoenix, not on the road home. No one knew better than I how late Penny usually worked. However, Pete himself was at the checkout stand, and he was kind enough to ring her at home for me.

"Hello, Penny?" I said, using Pete's phone

behind the counter. "I didn't wake you, did I?"

"Shucks, no. I was just watching a 'Dynasty' rerun. You follow that show? I love it. I love Joan Collins. She's such a bitch. How've you been keeping?"

"I've been keeping strange company, Penny. You remember that blond girl I had with me when I was in a couple of days ago?"

"Lord, yes! It's the strangest thing. I haven't been able to get her out of my mind. Don't tell me she's been staying with you? Oh, I bet Linda loves that."

"Yes, she has been staying with me. But Linda . . . hasn't really complained. Penny, why have you been thinking about her so much?"

"Well, she was so gorgeous. And sweet, too, I could see that right off. I just liked her a whole lot."

"When you first met her, you thought you'd seen her before. Had you?"

"She did look sort of familiar. I don't know—had we met, it seems I would have remembered her. She wasn't your ordinary gal."

"There was a man in the diner that night who seemed to recognize her," I said. "We've had coffee together a couple of times, but I can't remember his name. He's a foreman at a factory in Catson. Do you know who I'm talking about?"

"Do you mean Clyde Sheian?"

"That's him! Sheian, yeah. Do you know how I could get hold of him?"

"Try his work. That's Poll's Cardboard, in Catson. You can get their number from information. But Sheian probably won't be there now. He usually works late."

"I'll give it a shot."

"Wait, don't leave me like this! What's up? What's she done?"

"I'm sorry, Penny, it's a long story. We'll have to save it for another time."

I said goodbye and thanked Pete for the use of his phone. I moved to the phone booth outside. The factory's number was easy to obtain and Mr. Sheian was working, after all. He vaguely remembered me, but he was busy and wanted me to state my business. I told him about his staring at a blond I was with a couple of nights ago. The sound of his voice changed. He seemed to hold the phone closer to his mouth.

"Is she a friend of yours?" he asked.

"She's staying with me. But I don't know where she came from. I'm trying to see if she has any family around here." My heart was pounding. "Do you know her?"

"Why, yes, I think so. Her name's Kathy Lion. She used to live in a house I rented. I was surprised to see her in Pete's. Casey had told me she'd left town ten days ago."

"Who's Casey?" All of a sudden, I didn't feel so hot. And this was exactly the news I'd been looking for.

"She was Kathy's next-door neighbor. You really ought to talk to her. She knew Kathy best."

"Is her number listed?" I asked.

"Probably. Her last name's Barbers. Is some-

Christopher Pike

thing wrong with Kathy? She was such a spirited girl."

I swallowed, telling myself my disappointment was irrational, that as a lonely truck driver I couldn't expect to be picking up Goddesses in the middle of the night, that my expectations had simply been too high. It was only then I realized how much I wanted to believe Sati.

"No, she's fine," I said. "She's great. Do you know where she was going when she left?"

"Casey said she was headed to L.A. I understand she wanted to be an actress."

Casey Barbers wasn't the suspicious type. When I told her I was a friend of Kathy's, and in the neighborhood, she didn't hesitate to invite me by for tea. Only in small towns do you find strangers eager to make you tea.

The lady's street was narrow and in need of repair. My truck parked in front of her house practically closed off the road. The neighborhood had probably seen better days, but it didn't look like the sort of place earthshakers had ever emerged from. Somehow, I couldn't picture Sati walking its crummy sidewalks.

Casey Barbers was wiping grease from her hands with a napkin when she answered the door. Food must have been an all-day affair with her; she was fat. She was so fat I had to wonder how her poor heart could possibly pump blood to every one of her fat cells.

"Hi, Mr. Winters," she said. "You look exactly as I imagined you would on the phone."

"I'll take that as a compliment," I said.

"That's how it was given," she replied cheerfully, letting me in. "But I don't suppose I'm what you were expecting. I've had men ask me out without seeing me, just because of my telephone voice. It always cracks me up the way their faces fall when we meet." She closed the door and smiled at me with doughboy cheeks. She appeared to be around fifty, so I put her at thirty-five. "Have you had lunch, yet?"

Fat people always make me feel sad. I suppose it's because I feel no one would ever want them. Sometimes I wished Linda was fat so Dick wouldn't want her. But Linda just kept getting thinner, and more desirable.

"I've eaten, thank you," I said.

Miss Barbers nodded to Nick's sketch pad under my arm. "If you want to draw my picture, I hope you wouldn't mind coming back next week when I've finished my diet." She laughed at my discomfort. "You are a polite man, Mr. Winters, did anyone ever tell you that?"

"Sati told me that once," I replied, figuring I might as well get to the heart of the matter.

"Is that a girlfriend?" she asked, pointing me in the direction of the kitchen table. We sat down together.

"Not exactly." I uncovered Nick's handiwork and slid it toward her. "This is Sati."

Miss Barbers's expression brightened. "She's

157

pretty. She looks a lot like Kathy. Wait a second, what's going on here? Is Kathy using the stage name Sati?"

I leaned closer. "Miss Barbers, is this . . ."

"Please call me Casey."

"Casey, is this Kathy?"

"It looks like her. Don't you know?"

"No. That's my problem. I picked this girl up a few days ago just west of Catson. She told me her name was Sati. Since then, she's been staying at my place and . . . carrying on in an unusual fashion. Please study this drawing closely. I've got to know for sure if it's her or not."

"I'll need my glasses," Miss Barbers said, getting up again. "My contacts aren't strong enough."

"Yes, use your glasses." I was sweating, hanging onto a faint hope. But what was I hoping for, anyway? That Sati was God? Miss Barbers could only prove she wasn't. And I already knew that. Any fool knew that.

Back in her chair with her glasses, Miss Barbers studied the picture for a long time. "Yeah, this is Kathy," she said finally.

I closed my eyes for a second. "Are you absolutely sure? You stared at it for so long before saying anything."

"Well, it's a drawing. You should have brought me a photograph."

"She wouldn't let me take a photograph."

Miss Barbers giggled; her whole body did. "That's Kathy! She'd never pose for a picture.

158

And here she wanted to be famous. I'd tell her, 'Kathy, how can you be in the movies if you won't get in front of a camera?'" She tapped Nick's sketch. "I'm surprised you got her to sit for this."

"Does she have any family living in town?"

"No. She's from the Midwest. But don't ask me about her family. She never talked about them. For such a pleasant girl, she sure could be closed about certain things." The woman chuckled. "That's cute she's using a new name."

"How long have you known her?" I asked.

"Oh, six months. She lived right next door. But I didn't see her that often. She stayed inside most of the time. She worked at home."

"What did she do?"

"She was a writer," Casey said.

"What?"

"That's what I said when she told me. She used to sell short stories to all kinds of magazines. Oh, I just remembered, she always used pseudonyms. That explains it!"

"Explains what?"

"Why she's gone and made up a stage name. What last name has she adopted?"

"Sati's all she's going by," I replied dryly.

"That's Hollywood for you. But Mr. Winters, why did you say Kathy was carrying on in an unusual fashion? Has she done anything wrong?"

"She's saying she's God."

"Pardon?"

"She's saying she's God."

That took Miss Barbers back. "Why is she doing that?"

"I don't know," I said. "Do you?"

"No, I mean, I always thought she was a strange girl. Nice, you understand, very polite, but still strange. But I thought that was because she spent so much time writing." Miss Barbers frowned. "I hope the poor thing's not taking drugs."

"Did she ever give you a sample of her writing, anything she'd published?"

"No."

"Never?"

"No, and I asked her for a piece on several occasions. But I do know she wrote a lot of science fiction, fantasy and far-out stuff like that."

"Figures," I muttered. "Did she have a car?"

"No. She was going to hitchhike to L.A. I'm glad she got picked up by a nice man like you."

"When exactly did she leave?"

"You must know. It was last week."

I sat up. "Are you sure? Today's Wednesday. I only picked her up Monday, at two in the morning."

Miss Barbers frowned again. "That's odd. Of course, she could have left later without my knowing."

I rubbed my eyes. I was tired already, and I still had to get to Phoenix, drop my freight off and drive home. I wasn't looking forward to seeing Sati again, not the way I had been all the other times.

"Casey," I said. "Could you take one last look at this drawing and tell me, beyond a shadow of a doubt, that this is the Kathy Lion that you knew?"

Miss Barbers picked up the pad and held it at arm's length. Apparently, even with her glasses, her eyesight wasn't great. "If this isn't Kathy," she said, "I don't know who it is."

# Chapter 11

Procrastination and I are old friends. Instead of returning straight home after delivering my freight, I talked myself into finding a motel in Phoenix. I figured I'd stay overnight and scout prospective clients the next morning. I knew I was just putting off the inevitable. Still, I went so far as to get a room. I even had dinner, and killed a couple of hours with a ridiculously long walk. But when it was near ten, and time to lay my head on the pillow, I realized I wasn't going to be able to sleep until I talked to Sati. I got back in my truck and started on the all-night drive. I didn't pass a single hitchhiker on the road.

At home, I found Sati sitting out front with Fred, folding papers. Sunrise was a couple of hours away. L.A. never really slept, but the street was deserted, and it seemed very peaceful. I could hear the ocean waves breaking more than half a mile away. There was a chill in the air. Both Sati and Fred wore sweaters.

"How are you doing?" Fred asked, hardly glancing up, his voice flat.

"Tired," I muttered. "How are you?"

"Great," Fred said.

He was exaggerating, but I wasn't going to argue the point. Sati had set aside her rubber bands and was watching me, her hair tied up in a bun, looking in the dark like any other pretty young girl. Yet in the instant she turned her eyes on me, I knew I wouldn't be confronting her with my discovery. Suddenly, I couldn't bear the thought of calling her a liar, of ruining her fantasy. I, too, sometimes wished I was God. I guess everyone has at least once in their life.

"Hello, Sati," I said.

She nodded. "Michael."

"How are things?"

"Things are good," she said.

"I'm glad."

"Mike, I've got to talk to you alone," Fred said abruptly, standing up.

"Sure. See you later, Sati."

"OK."

Fred didn't say a word until we were inside my apartment. Then he exploded. "What's this I hear about you and Lori fooling around?"

"Who told you that?" I asked, flipping on the

lamp and plopping on the couch, more tired than any human being had a right to be.

"Lori told me!"

"Did you believe her?"

"I'm serious. I don't like this. I don't like this one bit."

I sighed. "What exactly did Lori tell you?"

Fred went to speak, stopped, stuck his hands in his pockets, and then pulled them back out again. "She said she made a pass at you!" His voice choked. "Why didn't you tell me, Mike?"

That didn't sound like the Lori I knew. "She told you that?"

"Yeah." His lip quivered. "Is it true?"

"Yes."

Fred slammed his fist into his leg. "Why didn't you tell me?"

He was hurting, and I felt bad for him. Yet, at the same time, I was pleased to hear of her confession. "I didn't want to upset you."

Fred began to pace. "I don't see how you could have kept this from me. All those times we talked together about Lori, and here you *knew* she wanted you instead of me!"

"She only made a pass at me a couple of days ago."

He stopped. "What about the time I left the two of you alone when my car broke down? What about that time, huh? That was a long time ago!"

"Oh, yeah. I'd forgotten about that."

He moved a step closer, shaking his finger. "Were you flirting with her?"

"No."

"Are you sure you didn't encourage her? You told me once how cute she was. I remember you telling me that."

"She is cute."

Fred slammed his fists in his legs again. "I knew it! I knew it! You *were* flirting with her!"

"Calm down, Fred. You're going to wake everyone up. No, I wasn't flirting with her. You know I wouldn't do that. Any suggestive remarks came strictly from her side."

Fred threw himself into the chair Sati had used for her first meeting. "Thanks for telling me that. That makes me feel great. Thanks a lot, Mike."

"I'm sorry."

Fred shook his head, close to crying. "What are you sorry about? She wasn't your girl-friend."

I let a couple of minutes of silence pass. Fred stared at the floor, sniffing occasionally. His fidgeting began to subside.

"Maybe this is for the best," I said finally, gently. "Maybe you would be better off with someone else. To tell you the truth, I've never thought Lori was your type. She's too . . . typical."

He snorted softly. "She's not typical any-more."

I paused, remembering her crying at Sati's meeting. "What do you mean?" I asked.

"She's totally changed. She says we have a lot of stuff between us that needs working out."

"Huh?"

Fred spoke to the floor. "She's made this list. It's full of all these problems we have."

"Wait a second. She's breaking up with you, right?"

Fred looked at me as if I was a moron. "No. Who told you that? I'm breaking up with her. She's been unfaithful. How could I possibly stay with her?"

"But Lori's been going out with other guys all along. You've known that."

"Yeah, but none of them was my best friend."

"What difference does that make?" I asked.

"It makes a lot of difference."

"But I never went out with her."

"That doesn't make any difference. She wanted to go out with you." He winced. "She told me she wanted to go to bed with you."

I scratched my head, figuring my fatigue must be to blame for my slow comprehension. "Doesn't she still want to go to bed with me?"

Fred convulsed in his seat. "Mike!"

"Shh. What I mean is, it sounds like she's opening up to you now, that she's finally willing to work at having a real relationship."

Fred glowered. "Swell. You're all heart, you know that? You're saying we *never* had a real relationship. Thanks a lot."

"This seems to me to be good news. You should be happy."

"Don't start sounding like Sati on me." He crossed his arms across his chest, pouted. "This whole mess is all her fault."

"Sati's?"

"Yeah."

"What did she do?"

"I don't know. She's God—how am I supposed to know what she's done?" He resettled himself into a more uncomfortable position. "I shouldn't have taken Lori to that meeting when that preacher tried to hammer that nail in Sati."

"Did seeing that change Lori?"

"You better believe it. Yesterday, Lori insisted we get to the meeting an hour early so we could get a seat in the front row."

"Then Lori thinks Sati is God?" I asked.

"What's wrong with you, Mike? Aren't you awake?"

"I'm beginning to wonder."

"Of course Lori thinks she's God. She saw how Sati kept smiling even when she was about to get nailed. How could anybody do that unless they were God?"

I rested my head in my hands. "Let me get this straight. You have a girl you have adored for the last year, who's finally willing to work through whatever may be keeping you two apart. And you have another girl, who's God, who's willing to help you deliver your papers. And you're still not happy?"

Fred thought about it for a moment, and by golly if something didn't click inside. "I guess you're right," he said. "I guess it's not that big a deal that she was flirting with you. When I stop and look at what's happening around here, it's pretty mind-boggling. It just upset me so much, you know, when Lori told me she'd always had a crush on you."

"I understand. I think I understand."

Fred stood, stretching. "I better get back out there and help Sati finish folding the papers. You look like you could use some sleep. Thanks for talking with me."

"No problem."

When he was gone, I called David. It was four-thirty in the morning and I knew I would be waking him. I didn't care. If I didn't have the heart to stop this madness, I was sure he would.

Wasn't I in for a surprise.

Five rings went by before he answered. "Hello?" he whispered. In the background, I could hear a female voice moan, "Who is it?" She sounded in her midteens.

"This is Mike," I said. "I know who Sati is."

He was instantly awake. "Who?"

"Kathy Lion. She's a free-lance writer who's lived in Catson for the last six months. I met her next-door neighbor yesterday. The neighbor said Kathy has always wanted to be an actress. What do you think of that?"

"I think that's very interesting."

"Interesting? Is that all?"

"Mike, could you hold on a minute? I want to change phones." He took two minutes. Listening on the line, I could hear the young girl swearing softly. Finally David picked up another phone and asked his darling to hang up her end. When we were finally alone, he said,

"I've got to tell you what went on last night. It was fantastic. Sati had another meeting and twice the number showed up. We had people sitting all over the floor. She took tons of questions and there wasn't one she didn't have the perfect answer for. There was even this physicist in the audience. The two of them had this great rap about how quantum mechanics is closing in on describing the ultimate reality."

"Dave . . ."

"I haven't told you the best part. There were a lot of people present who had come the night before. A couple got up and gave testimonials of healing! One old goat said his emphysema was much better, and this ugly chick told about how the swelling in her ankles had disappeared."

"Did Sati accept responsibility for healing the old goat and the ugly chick?" I asked.

"No. Her style is totally different from TV evangelists'. She acted as though the healings were of absolutely no importance."

"Why, then, do you think they're important?"

"Come off it, Mike. Spiritual people have to be healers if they want to have any kind of following."

"You come off it," I said. "Didn't you hear what I just told you? Sati wasn't born in the desert a few days ago. Her name's not really Sati. She's lied to us. She's not God. She's a fake."

"What's the big surprise? We knew she had to be somebody. If she's a Kathy or Gertrude or a Pamela, who gives a damn? As long as she thinks she's God and can play the part. That's all I care about. She's going to be big."

"What about launching ships that might sink? Sooner or later her real identity is going to come out. Then her precious meetings won't fill up the first row."

"That's where you're wrong," David said. "She's never stated publicly that she's only a few days old. No one's heard that except you. And who's to say Kathy Lion couldn't have been God all along? Jesus didn't start doing weird stuff till he was thirty. Up until then he was just Joe Carpenter."

"Dave, doesn't it strike you that there is a fundamental flaw in your whole reasoning? Sati is *not* who she says she is."

"Has she hurt anybody?" David asked.

"In a sense, yes. She's misled them."

"That's B.S., and you know it. People will always follow somebody. Why shouldn't they follow her? At least she doesn't steal their money or lay guilt trips on them for every time they have a horny thought. She helps people. I want to help her. If you don't want to go along, fine. Just don't ruin it for everyone else."

I didn't respond immediately. Not for an instant did I believe David's motives were altruistic. He had money, but lots of people have money. He wanted to be a *somebody*, and if that wasn't possible, he wanted to be in charge of a *somebody*. Yet there was a certain sense to his argument, never mind the fact that it was based on a lie. Sati *did* make people happy. Was I acting so self-righteous because I knew I could no longer be one of those people?

"All right, Dave," I said finally.

"You won't get up at her meetings and bring up that thing about her being born in the desert?"

"I won't be going to any more of her meetings."

"That's your decision," David said. "They keep getting bigger and better. Tonight's meeting is at the Unity Church, not far from the bank we've been using. The church minister heard her last night and was impressed. The place seats eight hundred. And I've talked to some people at the "L.A. in Focus" program. You know, the show that interviews folks who give L.A. its color? They're sending someone out tomorrow to hear her."

"Sati flat out told me she never wanted to be on TV."

"I discussed it with her. She didn't say no."

Suddenly, I had a splitting headache. "All right, whatever you say. I've got to go."

"Wait a sec. Give me the name of that neighbor you spoke to."

"What for?" I asked.

"Does it matter? I want to talk to her."

"Casey Barbers. She's in the book."

"Thanks. Cheer up, Mike. The way I see it, knowing she's not God makes what she does that much more impressive."

"Goodbye, Dave."

"Take care."

When I hung up, I noticed Sati standing in the doorway. "How long have you been there?" I asked.

She stepped inside. "Just a moment. I have to use the bathroom."

"God has to use a bathroom?"

"She does when she has a human body."

She hadn't overheard me, I decided. I didn't know if that was good or bad. "I hear your meeting was a big success."

She nodded. "Your daughter enjoyed the last one."

"Jenny was there?"

"Yes."

"She must be dragging her mother," I said.

"Linda brought her boyfriend last night."

"Dick?"

"Dick."

"Oh." I got up slowly. "I better hit the sack."

She touched my arm as I stepped by. "I'll have breakfast ready for you when you wake up."

"Pancakes?" I asked.

"Made with fresh milk. You still trust me as a cook, don't you, Michael?"

Sati stood only a couple of feet away, those eyes of hers almost big enough and blue enough to make me believe in Timmy's angel. Once more, I had an overpowering desire to hug her. To bury my face in her sunny hair. To ask her why. But the best I could do was lower my head.

"I trust you," I said.

173

# Chapter 12

It was Thursday, only four days since I had picked Sati up. A lot had happened in such a short time. I'd been charmed, zapped, poisoned, overwhelmed, and disillusioned. I figured I needed a break. I spent the next few days concentrating on my work.

Sati sensed my desire to be alone and stayed out of my way, quite a feat considering she was living with me in a cramped apartment. I didn't know why she continued to remain in my tiny place. Dozens of people who attended her meetings extended her invitations to move in with them. But not only did she turn them down, she asked that people please not visit her at my apartment. I suppose I should have been thankful for small favors.

Yet if Sati was content to leave me alone, Nick, Fred, and Jenny were not. They couldn't understand why I wasn't coming to the meetings. The excuse that I had to work did little to pacify them, especially when it came to my daughter. She comprehended perhaps a fraction of what Sati said, and it didn't matter. Sati made her happy. Sati chased away the nightmares. Sati was better than Santa Claus.

It was Nick, not Linda, who continued to take Jenny to the meetings. It seemed Dick had not taken to Sati, and apparently Linda felt they were entering a "delicate time" in their relationship. She didn't want to make waves. This talk of delicate Dick times troubled me. But I was scared to ask Linda what she was talking about.

Linda's qualms over Sati's influence on Jenny disappeared. I suppose getting to sleep through the entire night without being awakened by a frightened child had a strong effect on her outlook.

Nick would grab me between my comings and goings. The numbers at Sati's meetings were doubling every night, he said. At this rate, the whole world would be listening to her by midsummer. People left and right were being healed. Nick said the testimonials were unbelievable.

His remarks bothered me for opposing reasons. I knew now that the peace experienced during her periods of silence must have been due to suggestion. It was the only rational explanation. Yet I still missed those times. For whatever reason, they had made me feel better.

On the other hand, where were the real miracles? I would ask Nick that every time he stopped me. Just one paraplegic with a severed spine getting up and walking around the room was what I wanted. Instead, all I heard of were people experiencing relief from complaints that had largely psychosomatic origins: asthma, headaches, high blood pressure. Nick didn't argue the point with me. He wasn't a true believer, not like Fred. But he always had a gleam in his eyes when he spoke of Sati. I wondered if it wasn't just a question of time until he became like Fred.

I had to worry about Nick for business reasons as well. With the dough David had helped me borrow, I had put a down payment on one of the used tractors and trailers I had told the loan officer about. I was still negotiating on the other equipment, but there was little question that I'd soon be needing another two drivers. Nick was supposed to be one of them. He already had his Class 1 license. I now had solid deals for extra freight. The money would be there, and for whomever I hired, the pay would be steady.

Yet Nick had begun to have second thoughts. In addition to the job in Westwood, he'd picked up a fireplace to build in the valley. He felt things were looking up. I warned him that he couldn't count on it, especially with a pregnant girlfriend. But he wasn't listening. I hadn't realized how much he enjoyed working with his hands. Driving long distance, he confessed, reminded him too much of his dope-dealing days. Those days had been as recent as last week, but he looked at me as if I was nuts when I asked if he would ever return to pushing drugs.

Of course Sati was responsible for most of this. Faith has amazing power, I began to see, even when your God doesn't care if you believe in her or not. Several times I thought of addressing her as Kathy Lion when the others were present. But I never did, and I doubt if I thought about it that seriously. I was happy for everyone, I really was.

And I was miserable.

Early the following Wednesday morning, ten days after meeting Sati for the first time, I was coming down my stairs when I ran into Mrs. Hutchinson. Scissors and gloves in hand, she was working in her flower garden, using her fingers in ways that would have been unimaginable a couple of weeks ago. Seeing her this way, I had to stop and think how Casey Barbers had held Sati's picture at a distance to get a better look at it. Yet I refused to let myself hope. It had hurt too much to have the hope crushed the first time.

"If you start getting up any earlier, Mrs. Hutchinson," I said, "I'm going to use you as my alarm clock."

She stood quickly from her labors, standing remarkably straight for a woman of her age. "Mike, you startled me. Off to work?"

"Yeah, I've got to go to San Onofre and pick up some nuclear waste to dump in a redwood forest up north."

She laughed. "You're never serious, are you? I've missed you lately. Where have you been?"

"On the road, the usual." From Nick, I knew she was going to all of Sati's meetings. Yet he had had no idea whether Sati had changed her religious beliefs. "How have you been?" I asked.

"Wonderful!" She took a deep breath. "It's nice to be up at this time of day, just before the sun comes up. It's the only time to work."

"You do seem to be enjoying a strong second wind."

She knew what I was hinting at. Glancing self-consciously at her hands, she set aside her scissors and gloves. "You're right," she admitted quietly. "Sometimes I think it's a miracle."

"Really?"

"I know I had hard words for her in the beginning. I regret the things I said. Sati—she's not a bad person." Mrs. Hutchinson spoke seriously. "She's a wonderful person."

"But is she God?"

Mrs. Hutchinson reached out and touched the petal of an opening rose. "I'm going to pick these for her meeting tonight. She looks so beautiful with a flower in her hand." Mrs. Hutchinson shook her head. "What can I say, Mike? Before I always had a yes-or-no answer for everything. But here I've finally met this person who's completely at peace, and she doesn't care what I know. She says I have to learn to say I don't know. So I don't know anything, I guess, except that she's given me some of her peace. And that I thank the Lord for her coming."

"But she contradicts the Bible?" I asked.

"Does she? Oh, I guess she does. But I must tell you. I went home last night after her meeting and read the Gospel of John. The words of Jesus were different from her words, and yet I felt they were saying the same thing."

"And what was that?"

Mrs. Hutchinson stared at me with open eyes. "That I should rejoice, for the kingdom is at hand."

I shifted uncomfortably. "Have you spoken to Reverend Green about this?" I asked.

Her face tensed. She turned away. "I felt terrible that night. I had no idea what he had in his briefcase. When he almost hurt her hand, I didn't know if I'd ever be able to forgive him. But you've got to understand this, Mike, he's a fine person. He works long hours outside of his ministry duties. He helps runaway kids. He finds ways to get them off the streets. He'd do anything for you. He'd give you the shirt off his back if you needed it."

"Have you spoken to him recently?"

"No," she said. "I can't get hold of him. All I know is he has resigned as minister of our church."

"What?"

She nodded. "The church secretary said he

came in last Thursday and told her he was quitting."

"Did he give a reason?"

"Not really. But he said something about going surfing."

The talk was getting too strange for me. "Where is Sati right now?" I asked.

"I haven't seen her. I think she's still helping Fred deliver his papers."

"I better get going myself. Oh, have you seen Timmy lately? I keep missing him."

She glanced across the swimming pool, in the direction of Timmy's apartment. "I was going to check on him in a couple of hours. He wasn't at the meeting last night."

"How's his cough been?"

She brightened. "Much better. He says he's been sleeping like a baby every night. In fact, it was funny, he fell asleep during Sati's silence Monday night. When she asked us to open our eyes, he was snoring his head off."

"It's great that he's getting lots of rest."

"Yes." Mrs. Hutchinson paused. "But maybe that wasn't Monday night. No, I think it was Sunday." She frowned. "That was the last time I saw him. That's odd, he's missed two meetings in a row. And he enjoys them so much."

Suddenly, I felt uneasy. "What time does Timmy usually get up?" I asked.

She caught my drift immediately. "Usually between eight and nine. We'd be waking him if we called him now." She rubbed her hands together. "But I've wakened him before, and he's not minded."

I nodded. "Let's take the chance."

Timmy did not answer his doorbell. "Timmy," I called. "Timmy." Waiting can be so hard. "Timmy!"

"I should have checked on him yesterday," Mrs. Hutchinson said anxiously. "I meant to, but I helped Sati make cookies for her meeting, and then I forgot. Timmy!" She pounded on the door. "Timmy!"

I stopped her. "There's a better way. You have the master key to these apartments. Go get it."

Her face was a mask of concern. "Do you think he's too sick to get up? That must be it. And I forgot to check on him. Lord, forgive me. Timmy!"

I put my hands on her shoulders. "We'll get the key together. He's probably just in the shower or something. Everything's going to be all right."

I try to fool others almost as often as I try to fool myself. Fetching the key and opening the door, we found Timmy lying on the couch with the TV on low. At first I thought he was dead. He didn't respond when I shook him, and I shook him hard. His skin was clammy to touch but, leaning close, I could hear the faint sound of his wheezing breath.

"He's alive, isn't he?" Mrs. Hutchinson whispered, standing behind me. "Lord, he's got to be alive."

"Yes, he's going to be fine." I turned on the

lamp and checked in his mouth. Nothing was obstructing his breathing, except perhaps two heavily infected lungs. "Timmy!" I shouted. He didn't respond. I slapped him. To my immense relief, he sighed softly and opened his eyes.

"Mike," he croaked. "What time is it?"

"Time you saw a doctor." Bending over, I scooped him off the couch and cradled him in my arms. "My car's in front," I told Mrs. Hutchinson. "Wake Nick and tell him to meet me out there. One of us will have to hold him while the other drives."

"I can hold him," she cried, desperate to make up for whatever she felt she had failed to do.

"No, you can't, nor can you drive. But you can come with us. Just get Nick."

She turned for the door, then stopped. "Shouldn't we wait until Sati returns? She could look at him."

"No," I said.


I like doctors about as much as I like loan officers. The middle-aged M.D. who spoke to the three of us in the waiting room two hours after Timmy had been admitted somehow managed to appear both sympathetic and indifferent at the same time.

"I have bad news," he said bluntly. "X rays show his lungs almost completely blocked. We've ventilated him with oxygen, and he's now alert, but our options are limited. Lab says he has *Pneumocystis carinii*. It's a parasitic form of pneumonia often found in AIDS patients. It's got a strong hold on him. It responds poorly to antibiotics."

"Does it respond at all?" Nick asked.

"Not really," the doctor said. "Not when it's this far advanced."

"Are there any other forms of medication you can use?" I asked.

"There are, yes, but at this late a stage in the ballgame, I doubt they will be very effective."

"He's going to die?" Mrs. Hutchinson asked in disbelief.

"I'm afraid so," the doctor said.

She trembled. "But it was only Sunday he was feeling better than he had in months. How can he be dying?"

"With a crippled immune system, an infection can go wild in a matter of days," the doctor explained. "Hours, even."

"How long?" I asked.

The doctor shrugged. "He would do better if he would allow us to continue to ventilate him with a richer oxygen content. But he won't let us put him under an oxygen tent. In a way, it doesn't matter. He's not going to last long. I'm sorry I have to put it to you this way."

Mrs. Hutchinson began to cry. Nick wrapped an arm around her. "Can we see him?" I asked.

"He's in intensive care. Only immediate family is allowed in, and then only for brief periods."

"We're the only family he has," Nick said, his voice unsteady. "His parents despise him."

The doctor considered. "I'll have a word with the nurse. Try not to tire him."

The only time I had been in an intensive care environment had been in high school when my mother had had a heart attack. In that hospital, the beds had been separated by nothing more than curtains. Here each patient had his or her own cubicle, the rooms spaced in a half circle around a computer-equipped nurses' station that resembled a space shuttle control board. The nurse on duty reiterated the doctor's final instruction, and we were led to Timmy.

There were IVs in his arms and wires attached to his chest. His thin unwashed hair hung limp beside his pale face. My eyes stung at the sight of him, but I refused to cry. I had not cried since my mother died in my arms.

"How are you feeling?" I asked, taking his hand. The room was unusually warm but his fingers were cold. Before, no matter how sick he'd looked, there had always been laughter in his eyes. Now he had to strain to keep them open.

"OK," he whispered. "Thanks for bringing me in." He sucked in a short breath. "What's the doctor say?"

"He didn't talk to you?" I asked.

"No."

"He says if you keep your hands off us black boys you'll be just fine," Nick said.

Timmy smiled faintly. "Tell him I was in love

and couldn't help myself." He coughed. "What *did* he say?"

Had the roles been reversed, I would have wanted to know the truth. "You're sick, Timmy," I said. "Real sick."

He closed his eyes. "I feel sick."

Mrs. Hutchinson came to his side. "This is a wonderful hospital. They can help you. They're giving you some medication. You've just got to rest and get your strength back."

He smiled again, for her sake, though it was obvious he didn't believe her. "I will, Mrs. Hutchinson. I promise."

"Is there anything you need?" Nick asked.

Timmy looked up at him. "Yeah, I'd like to see Sati again before I . . . I can't see her. Is she around?"

"We'll get her for you," Nick said.

"Those gifts you helped me buy her," Timmy said. "They're in my bedroom. They're in a bag in the closet."

"I'll bring them," Nick said. "Anything else?"

He chuckled softly. "Oh, I don't know."

"What is it?" Nick insisted.

For an instant, he was his old devilish self. "Kiss me goodbye."

Nick didn't hesitate. He leaned over and gave Timmy a kiss on his forehead. "Now we'll be back, guy. You just stay right here."

Timmy nodded. "I will."

Taking the keys to my car, Nick and Mrs. Hutchinson left together to find Sati.

Timmy rested with his eyes closed for a

minute before speaking next. "This is the end of the road, isn't it, Mike?"

"It looks that way. Your lungs are pretty messed up."

"Must have been a draft," he said, joking. "But I had been feeling better. I'd been sleeping, and I'd been thinking maybe I was being cured." He coughed again, harder than last time, his white coloring taking on a blue tinge. When he stopped, he lay exhausted. It was a couple of minutes before he could continue. "Remember that story I told you about that redneck? How I took a lick of his ice-cream cone?"

"That was a great story," I said.

"I made it up."

"It doesn't matter."

He sighed. "I made it up because it was something I'd always wanted to do since I got sick. People like that are always saying how gays are just getting what they deserve. You probably never knew how much stuff like that bothered me."

"People like that are bastards, anyway. Let's not talk about them."

A tear started down his cheek. "I know I shouldn't care. It just hurts to know some people would rather see you dead. I never wanted to hurt anyone. I wouldn't have touched their ice cream." He struggled for breath. "I'm scared, Mike. I don't want to die."

I squeezed his hand. "I don't want you to die, either."

"I want to talk to my mom," he said suddenly.

"What?"

"My mom and dad. I haven't spoken to them in years."

"All right. I'll get hold of them for you. What's their number?"

"I don't know. I don't even know where they live now. But I have a cousin, Sally. She's in my black book at home. She should be able to get hold of them."

I stood. "I'll find them."

"Hurry," he said.

In the hallway outside intensive care, I rang Nick's apartment and got Mary. She ran over to Timmy's unlocked apartment and found Sally's number. The area code was 212—New York. I billed the call to my calling card. A young lady answered.

"Hello?"

"Hi," I said. "Is this Sally?"

"Yes."

"This is Michael Winters. You don't know me, but I'm a friend of your cousin, Timmy Pinton."

There was a long pause, then a giggle. "Sorry, I had to stretch my memory. I haven't seen Tim since we were kids. How is he?"

"He's in the hospital. He's very sick. The doctors say he's going to die."

"That's terrible," she said, distressed. "What's wrong with him?"

"He has pneumonia. He has AIDS."

"That's just awful. God."

"The reason I called—he wants to talk to his mom before he dies. Do you have a number where I can reach her?"

"I'm afraid I don't. They've moved recently, and I never got their new number. To be honest, Timmy's parents are not two of my favorite people. But I have relatives who might have it. Could I call you back?"

"Yes. I'm at the U.C.L.A. Medical Center. Offhand, I don't know the number here."

"I'll be able to get it. I'll have you paged."

"I appreciate this."

"Give Tim my best," she said. "He can call me collect, if he wants. If he's feeling up to it. I'm ashamed to say we hardly know each other."

We exchanged goodbyes and I hurried to tell Timmy what progress had been made. Unfortunately, the nurse said he was sleeping and wasn't to be disturbed. I sat down to wait.

Hours crawled by. By noon Timmy had failed to waken, and Sati had failed to arrive. Impatient, I called Nick's place again. He answered, and explained that he couldn't find her.

"How come she's not at my place baking cookies like she always is?" I complained. "Fred must have seen her last. What does he say?"

"When they finished delivering his papers, she told him she was going for a walk."

"How could she be taking a six-hour walk? Have you been out searching?"

"We've all been looking," Nick said. "I'm going back out now. But Sati often goes for long walks. No one knows where to. How's Timmy doing?"

"The same. Worse, maybe. Just find her. It'll break his heart if he has to die without seeing her again."

Nick lowered his voice. "Mary and the others are hoping Sati will heal him."

"That's insane," I said.

"Mike, I'm hoping the same myself."

What could I say? Putting down the phone, I silently cursed Casey Barbers. Had we never met, maybe I could have clung to the same impossible hope.

One o'clock came, followed by two and three, in the usual order. Timmy dreamed on. At a quarter to four, I heard myself paged. It was Sally. She apologized for the delay and gave me Timmy's parents' number. The area code indicated a town in Nebraska. But when I called, there was no answer.

Sitting and doing nothing has never been a strong suit with me. Now that I was no longer waiting for the phone number, I decided to join the search for Sati. I had no car, but I had money in my wallet and there were cabs sitting outside the hospital. Recalling her fondness for strolling along the water, I had myself dropped off at the beach.

The late afternoon was warm. For a weekday, there was a large number of people enjoying the sand and surf. Which direction to search was a toss-up. I headed north.

The sun had traveled several degrees closer to

the horizon by the time I found her. She was sitting alone, or rather, without human companionship. A flock of seagulls was gathered round her, accepting pieces of bread from her open hand. They flew away at my approach.

"Where have you been?" I demanded.

The orange sun was bright on her tan face. "Here."

"Timmy's in the hospital," I said. "He needs to see you."

She stood and brushed the sand from the pair of white pants Mary had loaned her. "I'll see him later," she said.

"You don't understand. There might not be a later. His lungs are about to fail."

"There's time," she said causally, stepping past me to the water. She let the foam wash over her bare feet. I followed, my impatience growing by leaps and bounds.

"Sati, I'm serious. He asked to see you. It's important to him."

She stared out to sea. "My meeting will be soon."

"Damn your meeting! I'm talking about Timmy. He's your friend."

"My friends will be at the meeting. All are equally dear to me."

I fought to control myself. "You won't come?"

Something far away seemed to hold her attention. "Tonight, I will be there for Timmy," she said softly.

"What if he dies before you get there?" I asked.

"He won't."

"But what if he does?"

"Then it's inevitable."

"Sati," I began, about to say something unkind. But then she looked at me, her blue eyes as calm as when she had looked across the table in the diner and told me she wasn't an actress. The words died in my throat. I turned and stalked off.

A cab took me back to the hospital. Mary, Fred, and Linda were now present, along with Nick and Mrs. Hutchinson. Nick said Timmy was awake, but that the nurse had asked them to wait outside while the doctor finished another examination. Nick carried a brown bag; presumably it held Sati's presents. I explained what Sati had told me. Linda was the only one who acted disgusted.

"She has a lot of nerve," she fumed.

"If she promised to be here later, what's the problem?" Fred asked. "That means Timmy won't die until later."

Linda glared at him. "I wouldn't count on it, kid."

I tried the number in Nebraska again, without success. The doctor finished his examination. His grim prognosis did not change. When he saw how many of us were waiting to visit with Timmy, he reminded us about the restrictions concerning intensive care patients.

"Look, why keep him hooked up to all that equipment?" I asked. "Move him to another room where he can visit with his friends and be happy with the time he has left."

"That would be against hospital procedure," the doctor said.

"Screw the procedure," Nick growled.

Without blinking, the doctor replied, "I say the same to myself several times a day. I'll see what can be done."

The time for Sati's meeting approached. Fred and Mrs. Hutchinson felt they should attend. The rest of us sat down for what was turning out to be an endless succession of waits. Linda stayed close to me, biting her nails.

"I left Jenny with Dick," she said. "I told her Timmy was sick."

"How did she take it?" I asked.

"She tried to reassure me. 'If he dies,' she said, 'Sati will take him to heaven where he can be with the angels forever.' Imagine, that was our daughter speaking."

The doctor did not return, but a nurse came by. In order for Timmy to be moved to an ordinary room, she informed us, he would have to be discharged and then readmitted. She mumbled something about insurance and lawsuits. Already worn out from all the red tape, Nick and I trudged downstairs and filled out the same forms we had filled out that morning. The phone in the Midwest continued to ring without an answer.

Close to ten, Nick and I were entering the elevator to go back upstairs when Sati called for us to hold the door. She was flanked by Fred,

Mrs. Hutchinson, and David. She had on a beautiful blue silk dress Mary had sewn especially for her meetings. In her arms was a huge bouquet of flowers. She looked positively radiant.

"I didn't think you'd make it," I said, relieved.

She crowded in with the others, her shoulder pressing against me. "I thought I would," she said.

In the waiting room, Mary and Linda had good news. The nurse had informed them Timmy had been moved to room 707. We could now talk to him as much as we wanted.

Timmy was propped up in bed when we entered. He looked better than he had in the morning, but perhaps it was from the joy of seeing his friends. His breathing and color were just as awful. Strangely enough, Sati stayed in the background while the rest of us joked with him. He kept his attention on whichever of us was talking, without even glancing her way. I understood. It was enough for him that she had come. Only once did he interrupt, to ask if I'd reached his mom. There was a phone next to his bed. I tried the number once more, but without luck.

"They'll be home soon," I told him.

Sometime in the midst of our visit, Timmy began to cough, and couldn't stop. Each time he sucked in the air, it bounced back out. We began to panic. I moved to call for a nurse when Sati—without a sign of haste—stepped to the sink and got him a glass of water. He was struggling so much he couldn't hold the cup without spilling. She lifted the water to his lips.

"A sip," she said. "Come on."

He managed to take a drink. His fit lasted a while longer before it finally subsided. I had never understood what it meant to die of pneumonia. Essentially he was slowly drowning. I realized I was drenched with sweat. Sati sat beside Timmy on the bed and shook her head.

"What am I going to do with you?" she asked.

"Heal me," he said, kidding.

"Is that what you want?" she asked.

The question embarrassed him. He changed the subject. "I got you something," he said.

"That's what I hear. I adore presents."

"Nick?" he said. Nick carefully set the bag on Timmy's lap. "This first gift isn't really for you, Sati," he went on, sticking his hand in the bag.

"Who's it for?" she asked.

"Me." He took out a book. It was the King James Version of the Bible. He let everyone see it, pleased at our confusion. He had his punch line ready. "I always said I wouldn't read the Bible until I got an autographed copy," he explained.

We enjoyed a good laugh. David brought forth a pen and Sati did the honors, simply writing her four-letter name on the inside cover. She had fine penmanship.

The next gift—and Timmy assured her this one was for her—was black lace lingerie. Even Sati waited for an explanation this time. Our patient didn't keep her in suspense. "You're the first woman I ever met that I found attractive." He added shyly, "I think you'd look pretty in these."

Sati smiled and held the sheer material up to her chest. "You flatter me," she said.

Timmy beamed. "Thanks for coming."

She leaned over and gave him a kiss on the lips. "Thanks for waiting for me."

He cleared his throat and briefly closed his eyes. His energy was beginning to ebb. "I know you don't like to talk about lives other than the one we're living now," he said. "But I've always believed in reincarnation. It's always made sense to me. Could there be something to it?"

"Could be," she said.

He spoke seriously. "If I do come back, will I be gay again? Will I still want men instead of women?"

Sati's eyes strayed to Mary, then back to Timmy. "If you were a beautiful girl," she said, "you could love all the boys, and no one would say boo to you."

The answer satisfied him. "I would like to live again," he whispered, sinking deeper into his pillows. "There's a lot of things I'd like . . ."

He didn't finish. He didn't start on another coughing fit, either. All of a sudden, he simply didn't have the air for words. Sati rolled him on his side so that he faced her, and calmly watched while the rest of us slowly freaked out. The raspy sound coming out his parched lips reminded me of the rattling of bones. There was death in the room. I could smell it as well as hear it.

As the seconds of struggle turned to minutes of torture, several in the room obviously began to feel it was time for Sati to shine forth her light. Fred and Mrs. Hutchinson kept exchanging frantic glances. But Sati continued to sit patiently, while Timmy smothered in her hands.

"I'm calling for help," I said finally, unable to take it any longer. I reached for the red button beside the bed. Fred leapt in my way.

"What are you doing?" he cried. "The doctors can't do anything for him!"

"I'll get someone myself, Mike," Linda said.

It was Mrs. Hutchinson's turn. She blocked Linda's path. "They've already told us they can't help him," the old woman said.

"Get out of my way!" Linda ordered.

"No!" Mrs. Hutchinson said, her whole body quivering.

"What's wrong with you two?" I demanded, still trying to get past Fred. "Can't you see he needs oxygen?"

"He needs more than oxygen," Fred said.

"For Christ's sake," Linda swore, unable to believe a seventy-year-old woman was physically trying to stop her. Any second, I thought, one of us was going to have to use some muscle.

"You're not bringing those people in here," Mrs. Hutchinson said.

"Fred," I began.

"No, Mike," Fred said, vigorously shaking his head.

"Nick," I said.

Linda threw up her arms, exasperated. "Dammit, what do you people want?"

Nick answered in a soft voice. "A miracle."

The hostilities ceased. All eyes went to Sati. And we waited, as all men had waited, throughout time, when they were hoping for divine intervention. Even Timmy, who was having a bad time of it, watched her. Sati let her gaze slip over each of us.

"Is this what you want?" she asked finally.

"What are you saying?" I asked.

"Do you want me to heal him?" Sati asked.

"Yeah!" Fred said. "Yeah!"

"Mary?" Sati said.

"I have faith in you," Mary said.

Sati looked to Nick. "Definitely," he said.

Mrs. Hutchinson hurried to her side and grabbed her hands, going down on her knees. "Do what you can for him, Sati. He's only a young man. He's been like a son to me."

"David?" she asked.

As Sati had done in the beginning, David had continued to do. He remained in the background, saying little. Now he appeared to want to get even farther away. He pressed his back to the far wall.

"Yes, help him," he muttered. "If you can."

"Linda?" Sati asked.

Linda stood frozen. "You can't help him," she whispered.

"I can do anything."

Linda stared at suffering Timmy. She nodded. "Then do it."

"Michael?" Sati asked.

She had often spoken of the limitation of our words, even our thoughts. And it was true I could find nothing inside me that could understand what she could do for Timmy. Yet suddenly Casey Barbers was forgotten. In that instant, many bizarre things seemed possible. "Do whatever you think is best," I said.

She accepted my response and turned at last to Timmy. She brushed her hand across his forehead. From the moment she had made her offer, his breathing had eased somewhat. The ghastly color of his skin, however, had not improved.

"What do you think is best, Timothy?" she asked.

"You could help me breathe?" he gasped.

"I could have you walk out of this hospital, and never be sick another day in your life."

"Really?"

"Yes."

He coughed, nodding. "I know."

She continued to run her fingers through his hair. "Whatever you ask of me, I will do for you," she said.

"But you didn't want to perform any miracles. You said . . ." He coughed again, and again. "You said that wasn't why you had come."

"I did say that," Sati agreed.

He strained for several seconds over what was being offered. Then he relaxed and shook his head. "I don't want to have anyone say you went back on your word. I don't want to take advantage of you."

"Let her help you!" Mrs. Hutchinson pleaded.

Sati repeated herself. "Anything you ask, Timothy."

He looked long in her face. Finally he smiled. "I wanted to see my mother again. That's all I really wanted." He leaned back and closed his eyes. "You don't have to heal me."

"Timmy!" I cried.

His expression was dreamy, far away. "It's all right now, Mike. I'm not afraid. I want to go on. I'm actually looking forward to it."

"Leave us alone," Sati said.

We did as we were told.

Out in the hallway, I found a pay phone. I dialed the number in Nebraska once more. I finally struck gold. An elderly lady picked up the phone.

"Hello?" she said.

"Hi. Is this Mrs. Pinton?"

"Who is this?"

"I'm a friend of your son. My name's Michael Winters."

She was suspicious. "What do you want?"

"Your son is in the hospital. He could die any minute. He wants to talk to you."

"Who are you? Is this a crank call?"

"I told you who I am. This is real. Please, talk to him. He's your own son, for God's sake."

Mrs. Pinton paused. "Is Timothy really dying?"

"Yes."

She had to think some more. "I'll talk to him," she said finally.

"Good. I'm not in his room, but it's only around the corner. I'll call you from there in a moment. Don't go away."

Excited, I ran back toward 707, passing the others, who were gathered in a silent group near the door. I had my hand on the knob when Sati came out.

"I've found his mom," I shouted. "Let me by."

Her blue eyes were clear and steady. As always. "He's dead," she said.

"What?"

"He's dead," she repeated. She turned to David. "Do you want to take me home?"

David backed up a step, shaken by the news. "No. I should stay. The hospital will have to be paid."

Sati nodded, unconcerned, holding a single rose from the bouquet of flowers she had brought with her. "You take me, Fred," she said.

Fred's eyes swelled with tears. "Why did you let him die?"

"All who are born, die," she said. "It is the way of things. Timothy's death is no reason for grief."

"But he never got to speak to his mother," I complained.

Sati gave me her flower. "Yes, he did, Michael."

Then she walked away, leaving us in grief it seemed we had every reason in the world to feel.

# Chapter 13

We ended up having a wedding instead of a funeral. The day after Timmy left us, Nick announced that he and Mary were getting married. Timmy's death, he told me, had somehow made it clear that being with Mary for the rest of his life was what he wanted.

Plans were made quickly. Mary spoke of a church wedding. Nick was interested in driving to Las Vegas. Sati suggested having the ceremony at sea. The couple laughed at the idea and went searching for a boat to rent.

The day of the ceremony was warm and clear, as each day had been since Sati entered our lives. The calm ocean rocked the hull of our ship with gentle hands. Everyone who had been at the hospital was on board with the exception of David, who couldn't be found anywhere. Jenny was also present. She was to be the couple's flower girl, or at least that was what Mary had told her. No one knew what Sati had planned.

Sati held the vase containing Timmy's ashes. When we were three miles from shore, she bade me cut the engine. She had us sit around her in a circle at the rear of the boat. With us watching in silence, without a word about Timmy's life, she removed the top from the vase and sprinkled his ashes in the blue water. When she was done, she submerged the container momentarily. Then she reached for the flute that had belonged to Timmy.

"If you wish, you may keep your eyes open for my song," she said.

The remark might have been a challenge. Sati could play the flute like no one I'd ever met, and the melody reminded me of none I had ever heard before. It was extraordinarily soothing. Staring at her as she sat on the side of the boat, the instrument close to her lips, her bright hair blowing in the light breeze, my eyes grew so heavy I was compelled to close them. Perhaps it was simple exhaustion. I hadn't slept two hours since Timmy had died. Whenever I did try to sleep, I felt as if something heavy was pressing down on top of me. I couldn't get the final wheezing sound of Timmy's lungs out of my head.

Except for now. Listening to Sati's song, it

was easy to forget my own life, never mind the loss of the life of another. The charm was different from her periods of silence. Here the peace rolled in waves, rather than expanding into nothingness. From out of nowhere, colors mixed with my thoughts, reds and blues my mind could almost taste. Our boat drifted on the water, and I drifted with it, to places I did not know.

When Sati stopped playing, I returned to my body with a pang.

"Open your eyes," she said. I did so, and checked on the others. They all appeared to be returning from the same waking dream.

Nick and Mary sat on either side of Sati. Sati reached out and joined their hands together, placing her own hands on top. Nick and Mary had gone down to city hall that morning and had made it all legal. But from the looks on their faces, it was now that they were to be married. Sati's ceremony proved to be the shortest on the books.

"You two have the blessings of Sati," she said. "You will live long and happy lives together. My eyes will always be on you. Now exchange rings and kisses."

We had wedding cookies in place of a wedding cake. They were from a secret recipe we were all familiar with. They still tasted good.

Sati had a meeting to give that evening. After a couple of hours on the water, we turned the boat toward the marina. We docked and everyone ran off to change for the lecture. I was left behind to tidy up the ship. I was about through when Linda returned.

"Jenny's with Mrs. Hutchinson," she said.

Linda's hair was in a ponytail. I was reminded of the days when she had been a cheerleader, when I used to admire her from the last row in the high school gym. I was happy she had returned to see me.

"It was a nice day for a wedding," I said.

"Nice day for a funeral," Linda said.

"Did it bother you that Sati didn't say anything?"

Linda shook her head and stepped into the boat. She sat near the cabin. "I thought what she did was perfect. Her song was lovely. Timmy always wanted to play the flute like that."

"I think the greatest flute player in the world wishes he could play the flute like that," I said.

Linda sighed. "I miss him."

I nodded and sat beside her. "I'm always going to miss him."

Linda looked at me. "You hold on to things longer than most of us. Do you know that?"

"You would know."

"I've got something to tell you. You won't like it."

"You got me the wrong birthday card?" I asked.

"No." She lowered her head. "Dick and I are getting married."

"Oh. What?"

"I said we're getting married."

"I heard you," I said.

"I didn't want to have to tell you today."

"That's OK. Like you said, it's a nice day for a funeral." The reds and blues in my mind turned gray. The sound of Timmy's choking returned, stronger than ever. I could hardly breathe. So I laughed instead. "You're kidding," I said.

"I'm not. I love him."

"Who?"

"Dick."

"I thought you loved me?"

She looked at me, her face miserable. "I don't anymore, Mike. I haven't loved you in a long time."

During the hundreds of hours we had talked since we had separated, she had never told me that. We had talked and talked and she had never said a damn word about love, or the lack of it.

"Congratulations," I said.

"We'll still be friends. You can see Jenny whenever you want."

"Does Jenny know?" My pain was as much for my daughter as for myself. I knew that before she went to sleep each night, she prayed that I would be coming home.

"I'll tell her soon," Linda said.

"No. Let me tell her."

"If you want. You don't hate me, do you?"

"Give me your ring."

"My ring?" She glanced at her hand. "I thought I would keep it and have it altered to fit my small finger."

"No. I want it back."

"Why?"

"Because it's mine. Because I paid for it."

She shook her head. She wanted to discuss the situation. I shook my head. She saw I was serious. She gave me the ring. I got up and walked away.

I was sitting on the beach, a couple of miles from the marina, when Sati found me. The sun had recently set and the sand was getting cold. She had changed clothes from our afternoon boat ride, into a nice long dress. I didn't really wonder how she had found me. She had a knack for such things, for everything.

"Doesn't your meeting start soon?" I asked as she sat down beside me.

"There's time." She paused. "Linda was concerned about you."

"I seriously doubt that my welfare is her primary concern."

"That is true."

"I see you've come to cheer me up," I said.

"I've come to give you a ride home. You'll recall that you came with Linda." She gestured over her shoulder. "I've got your truck."

"I hate that truck."

"Then get rid of it."

"Should I?" I asked. "If it wasn't for that truck, I wouldn't have found you."

"But you did find me. It's served its purpose."

I looked at her, then hid my face in my folded knees. I liked my face there. It was safe. "You're wrong, you know, when you say life is bliss," I said. "Life sucks."

"The waves on my ocean are often turbulent for those without an anchor. Until you find your anchor, you'll always be prone to seasickness."

"Thanks for the philosophy. It doesn't do a thing for me."

"Isn't that how it is with words and beliefs? They're only useful when you don't need them. They're not like me. You need a ride home and here I am." She put her arm around me and softened her tone. "Tell me, Michael?"

I raised my head and watched as birds practiced sky dives over the darkening water. I had a lump in my throat that was ready to crack into tears and humiliate me. I had only met her a few days ago. I hardly knew her.

Yet I told her what I had never told anyone before, not even Linda.

"I was a senior in high school when my mother died. Nick's mother died then, too. We played in a band together, but I think the real reason we became friends was because we had both just lost our moms. It was Nick who talked me into asking Linda out. I couldn't believe it when she said yes. I was the happiest person in the world. Then we started dating. More than anyone else, she helped me get over losing my mom." I stopped and picked up a handful of sand. "I guess I need a woman in my life, someone who loves me. Maybe we all do. In the end, even Timmy was looking for his mother." I swallowed thickly and dropped the sand.

"But now Timmy's dead, and Nick's married, and Linda's getting married, and here I am. And . . ." My voice choked. Sati said it for me.

"And here you are and you have no mother?"

"Yes." I looked at her. "What were you trying tell me at the hospital when you came out of Timmy's room?"

"Our first night together," Sati said, "you asked what I was doing in the desert before you arrived."

"You said you were waiting for me."

Sati nodded. "Yes. And now you know why."

I did not understand what she meant. Nevertheless, when she hugged me with both her arms, I buried my face in her hair and cried as I hadn't done in years. I felt like a small boy again. I felt better.

# Chapter 14

I awoke the next morning to discover two females sitting on my bed. Sati was down near my feet. Jenny was bouncing beside my head. Both had on shorts and T-shirts. Both were amused.

"Get up, daddy," Jenny said. "Sati needs help."

"Man helps the God who helps herself," I muttered, glancing at the clock. It was ten-fifteen. I'd slept ten hours straight without even knowing I was alive. Sati had taken me straight from the beach to her meeting at the Unity Church. Nick had been right about the crowds. The pews were jammed. Sati's period of silence at the beginning of the talk had been extremely relaxing. I blamed it for my long sleep.

"People will be coming to meet with me today," Sati said. "We need to clean out your storage room."

I sat up, looking for my robe. "Why not meet with them in the living room? It will take us all day to clean the junk out of that room. Besides, I have nowhere else to put the stuff."

"Nick and Mary left for the mountains this morning," Sati said. "They said we could move your things into their apartment."

"Why not just use their apartment?" I asked. "What's so special about that room?"

"It has a glorious view of the pool," Sati said.

"Who are these people?" The previous night, a couple of David's TV reporters had spoken to Sati. They wanted to film one of her lectures. But Sati had announced to the audience that there would be no meeting tonight. She hadn't explained why. I wondered if she was trying to discourage the press. Certainly, she hadn't let them pin her down as to when she would be available.

"They're three wise men!" Jenny said, excited. "It will be just like it was in the movie."

"What movie?" I asked.

Sati nodded. "You will recognize one of them, Michael. But as I have already explained to Jenny, no one is to be told who it was that visited me today."

"Why not?" I asked.

"The world is happy to embrace certain teachings, as long as they remain in their proper place. Each of the men who visits me today contributes to the welfare of mankind, but they work in entirely different ways. But that is only an illusion. Those they are associated with would be upset to know these men actually work together. That they work for me."

"Sounds mysterious," I said, although I was intrigued that a celebrity would be coming to see Sati. Again, I had to ask myself that most dangerous of all questions: *why?*

Sati stood. "Take your shower. We have much work to do."

"But I have to pick up some freight," I said. Sati gave me a look. "Don't tell me—Jesse has already gone for it?"

"Of course. What would you like for breakfast?"

"Do I have a choice other than pancakes?"

"No," Sati said.

"I'll have pancakes," I said.

When Sati had gone, I put on my robe. Jenny was watching me. "Are you sad, daddy?" she asked.

"No, I feel good," I replied, before I realized I wasn't lying, as I ordinarily would have done in such a situation. The whole world was caving in on me and my daughter was worried about my mental health. Yet I felt just fine. The meeting the previous night had done wonders to lift my spirits, even though Sati hadn't said a thing she hadn't said a dozen times before. I scooped Jenny into my arms. "Are you sad?" I asked.

"Mommy told me she was marrying Dick, but

I'm not sad." She hugged me. "Sati promised me you would never leave me."

"She knows what she's talking about, angel."

In the shower, I tried to wash off my doubts. But I was scrubbing backward. What I was really doing was doubting my doubts. I was beginning to think I might have put too much faith in Nick's sketch, or in Casey Barbers's eyesight. I couldn't get over how Sati had had the nerve to hold a dying man's hand and ask him if he wanted to be healed. I had to bring Casey Barbers to Sati, I decided, or vice versa. I had to know.

The pancakes were as tasty as always. However, I wasn't given a chance to savor them. When I was halfway through my stack, Sati started moving the smaller articles out of the storage room. I had never seen her so busy.

I don't really collect stuff, but I don't throw it away, either. I wished we had Nick's strong arms to help us. For some reason, when I moved out of the house, we'd had two TVs, two sofas, and two refrigerators. Now what does anyone need with two refrigerators? To make the situation even more ridiculous, my apartment was already equipped with its own refrigerator.

Fortunately, Sati had a strong back and didn't mind sweating. We had a riot of a time getting the spare refrigerator downstairs. The blasted thing had gone through the door when I moved in, but it must have grown since. It didn't matter how we tilted it—upside down, backward—it refused to leave the room. Finally, Sati suggested we take it through the window.

"But we're on the second floor," I protested.

"Don't worry," Sati said.

I took the window off and we gave Sati's plan a try. Ten minutes later, we had the icebox hanging halfway into the great outdoors when I stopped and asked Sati, "Now what?"

Sati glanced below and came around behind the refrigerator. Before I could stop her, she gave it a single hard shove.

"Wait!" I yelled. The appliance slid through my unprepared fingers and disappeared. "What did you do that for?"

Sati told me to look below. The icebox had landed on a row of bushes without so much as a thud. "It's probably scratched," I growled.

"The Goodwill doesn't mind a few scratches," Sati said.

"The Goodwill?"

"I called them this morning. I gave them Nick's apartment number. They'll be out tomorrow."

"But . . ."

"You don't need all this stuff," Sati said. "And you didn't think I was going to help you move it all back upstairs, did you?"

I could have blown up. I laughed instead. She was right.

When the room was clear, our job was only half done. The walls were filthy with scuff marks. We kept Jenny busy running for fresh buckets of soapy water while we washed them down. Sati muttered something about a new paint job being better and I offered to go for a couple of cans of paint. But then she didn't want the smell. I was anxious to meet these three characters.

We covered the floor with a beautiful carpet taken from Timmy's bedroom and brought in two living-room chairs, which Sati draped with clean sheets. Her serene expression showed signs of excitement.

"When are they coming?" I asked.

"The first one will be here in an hour."

"They're not coming together?"

"No." She paused. "We need flowers. You and Jennifer get some while I take a shower and change."

"OK," I said. "Anything else?"

"Don't ask them any questions. Keep your voices down when I am alone with them."

"How do they know you're here?" I asked.

Sati smiled. "Jennifer already told you. They're wise men."

Jenny and I ended up getting four different bouquets, just to be on the safe side. I began to wish Sati *had* started a religion. It would have been nice to write off the cost of all the flowers on my income tax.

Returning, we found Sati wearing the white dress she'd had on when I picked her up in the desert. To my knowledge, this was the first time she had worn it since Mary loaned her some of her own clothes. She wanted Jenny and me looking our best, too. She rummaged through the closet for a dress for my daughter, while I was *told* to take a second shower. When I came out, I found my only suit pressed and lying across my bed. It was another hot day, but I put the clothes on without complaint.

The first gentleman arrived at three o'clock.

He was an old Italian priest. He may even have been more than a priest, a cardinal or something. He wore a red sash around his waist, over his black gown, and had with him a couple of younger priests. The latter were also Italian. They did not actually enter the apartment. They only accompanied their superior to the door before departing, presumably to wait nearby. The old priest was carrying a handful of flowers.

We were arranged in a line, as Sati had instructed, with me closest to the door and Jenny on my right side. The priest shook my hand. He had quite a grip for an old fellow.

"*Buona sera,*" he said. "*Dio benedire tu.*"

"Pleased to meet you, father," I said.

"He's not your daddy," Jenny whispered, confused. Then the priest leaned over, with a twinkle in his eyes, and shook her hand. My daughter gave him a sweet grin and tried to mimic his Italian greeting.

"Blame Sara," she said.

The priest was in obvious awe of Sati. With great reverence, he bowed his head low and presented her with his flowers. She accepted them gracefully, smiling to put him at ease.

"*Buon benvenuto al casa nostra, padre,*" she

said, with an excellent accent. She took him by the arm and led him toward the room with the glorious view of the pool. They disappeared behind the closed door. Jenny and I retreated to the kitchen and entertained ourselves with games of checkers. Jenny won twice, but then, she cheated.

Why, I kept asking myself, would a cardinal come all the way to America to speak to Kathy Lion?

The gentleman was in and out in thirty minutes. His assistants showed up as if on cue. They escorted him back down the stairs. He waved goodbye to the three of us as he rounded the pool.

"Nice man," Jenny said.

"Very nice," Sati agreed.

"How did your meeting go?" I asked.

"Everything I do goes perfectly."

"All right," I said.

The next visitor arrived at five o'clock.

He was a tall, powerfully built African man. He came alone, and the surety with which he carried himself, the fierce intensity behind his dark eyes, was intimidating. His age was difficult to guess. Forty to sixty was in the ballpark. He wore white pants beneath a knee-length orange tunic. His long, braided hair did nothing to hide his massive skull. He hardly acknowledged Jenny or me. But he'd brought a garland of flowers, and with a deep bow he placed it around Sati's neck. She seemed in a hurry to get him away from us. Indeed, as she ushered him into the room, she suggested we go for a walk. She cautioned, however, that we must be back in an hour.

We walked to the beach. Jenny didn't like leaving Sati alone with the man. At the same time, she was glad to be away from him. He had impressed her the same way he had me, as a violent man, a man from another time even, when noble warriors weren't much different from savages. I wondered if he was a shaman of some kind.

He was gone when we returned. Sati was rearranging the flowers in the meeting room so that they stood around one chair alone.

"You have an unusual mixture of friends," I told her.

"You noticed," she said with a laugh, before lowering her voice and adding seriously. "Just be happy he's on our side."

"Who was he?"

"You mean, *what* was he."

"Huh?"

"The world is a lot stranger than you can imagine."

"Huh?

"Never mind," Sati said. "Our next guest will arrive shortly. He is very important to the world. While he is here, stay in the apartment. It's a great blessing to be near him."

"How can he bless us when we've got God making us breakfast?" I asked. Sati did not laugh at my joke.

"Wait till he gets here. You'll see."

She must have been concerned that our vibes were not up to par. Before the man arrived, she had us sit on the couch with our eyes closed and zapped us with an abbreviated period of silence. In our hands were flowers taken from the bouquets. These we were to offer to the man, she said.

Obviously, this last guy was to be the heaviest of all. With Sati sitting between me and Jenny, I settled immediately, happy for the extra session. After approximately ten minutes of deep rest, I began to notice an approaching presence.

Sati's periods of silence always had the effect of making me feel there was something great inside that I wasn't usually aware of. This approaching presence had a similar effect, only it was stronger. It grew in intensity so quickly and so concretely that my rational mind found it impossible to deny that something inexplicable by any set of scientific equations was transpiring. Yet I was not frightened. The presence was as comforting as Sati's warm hug on the beach. In a way, I felt I was experiencing another form of the same hug.

"He comes," Sati whispered.

Jenny and I opened our eyes. Sati was already on her feet, opening the door. She told us to stay where we were when we started to get up. "We have a minute," she said.

"Is this guy a *who* or a *what*?" I asked, and I was not being facetious. The silent buzz inside my head had not been broken by the opening of my eyes. Jenny looked as if a light had gone on inside her.

Sati hurried back to us, her face flushed.

"He is someone who knows me, who has become me," she said. "For such people, I become a slave."

"But if you're God, how could anyone be above you?"

"I am the goal, but only someone such as he can take you to the goal."

"He is one of these masters you spoke of at your meetings?" I asked.

"Yes."

"Is he nice?" Jenny asked.

"You'll love him," Sati said.

Sati arranged us next to the door, in the same order as before. Had I not been drunk with invisible euphoria, I might have trembled in my shoes. Through the door, I glimpsed a small Indian monk in a white dhoti coming up the stairs. He was followed by a young blond fellow in a navy blue suit. I recognized the monk immediately. I'll leave it at that.

"Michael," he said as he accepted my flowers. His voice was high and musical, his dark eyes enchanting. I remembered Sati's remark about how to find a good teacher, how they would remind one of her. The man could've been Sati's spiritual father.

"Welcome," I said, nodding.

Jenny held her flowers up, her palms pressed together. "Hi," she said shyly.

The monk smiled sweetly and took her flowers. He gave her a white rose in return. Then he moved on to Sati.

After watching how the others had bowed to her, I saw with some amazement that she lowered her head to him. Sati gave him a single white carnation. The monk accepted her behavior as perfectly natural. He said a few words in what I assumed was Hindi or some such Indian language. Sati replied in the same language. But this time she did not take her guest by the arm. She simply nodded in the direction of the meeting room. As he followed her, the monk looked back at me, and I don't think I am exaggerating to say that his eyes seemed to see to the depths of my being. I felt totally exposed yet, at the same time, totally safe. What I mean is, I was not ashamed.

"You've done well, Michael," he said.

And I felt, with my whole life, I had done just fine. It was a wonderful feeling.

The door closed and Jenny and I sat down. The monk's companion sat across from us. "Do you have any ice cream?" he asked.

"No," I answered softly, remembering Sati's instruction. "But we have cookies that Sati's made. Would you like one?"

"Sure."

"Jenny, would you get the pink box at the bottom of the icebox?" She jumped to obey.

"Is Sati the name of that young woman?" the guy asked.

"Yes. Didn't you know?"

"No. Who is she?"

"She's God."

"Come again?"

"She says she's God."

The guy didn't know what to make of that. I was pleased to see he was as ordinary as the rest of us. He took a bite out of one of the cookies Jenny brought him. "She should open a bakery," he remarked.

"I'm glad you like them." Sati hadn't forbidden me to question the monk's assistant. "Do you know why you're here?" I asked.

"No."

I gestured in the direction of the closed door. "*He* didn't say anything?"

"Nope. One minute we're on our way to South America, and the next, we're heading to L.A."

I leaned forward. "Does it always feel so heavy around him?"

He nodded. "Always."

Sati's cookies were usually capable of satisfying anybody's sweet tooth, but this guy wanted ice cream and I guess that was that. I told him about a joint down the block that made their own. He was out the door in a minute, with a promise to bring us back a pint of chocolate chip.

I didn't know if the vibes were wearing me out or what, but I began to feel drowsy. My daughter felt the same way.

"Could I lie down, daddy?" she asked, yawning.

"I don't think Sati or her guest would mind."

Christopher Pike

She stretched out on the couch and closed her eyes. I did not plan to join her. I simply reached a point where I knew I'd faint if I didn't put my head down. I think I was out before my head touched the sofa pillow.

The dream seemed to start immediately.

*The town was small and cozy. Everyone knew one another. There was one barbershop and one bakery. The local sheriff spent his days helping the local fireman rescue pets stuck in trees. The sun shone most of the time. This was my hometown.*

*I was twelve years old. Summer vacation had just begun. My friends and I were playing baseball. We played baseball all day and we never got tired of it.*

*Nick and Timmy were my best friends. We were usually on the same team, but we didn't always win. The other team had a fantastic pitcher. That was David. He could whiz a pitch by your bat and you'd feel the breeze before you'd see the ball. More than anything, we loved to get a hit off David. When we did, he would get furious.*

*A game was going on right now. It was half over and we were losing by a run. Nick was up at bat. Even though he was only a kid, he was big and strong. There were two outs. David threw him a couple of fastballs, and got him for two strikes. Then Nick connected on the third pitch and drove the ball hard up the left-field line. Timmy and I cheered. Nick went to second base.*

*It was my turn to bat. I knew I could either win the game or lose it. As I stepped up to hit, my*

224

mother called encouragement from the stands. Every day, without exception, she came to watch me play.

There wasn't a pitch David couldn't throw: curves, sliders, fastballs—he knew them all. I knew the only way to beat him was to be patient. Usually, on his first pitch, he gave you garbage.

Unfortunately, this time he put it right over the plate. I watched it go by. It was the second pitch that was no good, and I went for that one. Before I knew it, I had two strikes on me. The pressure was intense.

The third pitch was a curve ball. I got a piece of it, but not enough. The right fielder only had to jog a couple of steps to the side to catch my fly ball. The inning was over. David laughed at me as I walked back to the dugout. I was disappointed. Timmy patted me on the back.

"We'll get him next time," he said.

Before I went back onto the field—I played shortstop and I was pretty hot—my mother called to me. I jogged over to the bleachers.

"I should never have swung at that last pitch," I complained.

"You hit it far," she said, brushing the dust off my shirt.

"I should have hit it farther. I've got to get a home run or we'll lose."

She smiled. "There's time, Michael."

"I wish Dave wouldn't laugh at me when I strike out. I don't like that."

"Have him on your team next time."

"Dave? Ugh! He's gross. I've got to go, mom."

*She kissed me quickly. "Good luck."*

And then it was later in the game, in the bottom of the ninth inning, and the score was tied. I was up at bat again, and once again I had two strikes on me. David was already laughing. He thought he had me. I gripped the bat tightly. I would sock it out of the park, I swore to myself.

David threw a fastball, right at me. I saw it coming my way, but I didn't have a chance to move. It hit me hard on the knee, and I fell to the ground in pain. Timmy ran over and helped me up. I went to shout something dirty at David, but Timmy stopped me.

"You're on base," he said. "Let me bat and I'll knock you in."

Timmy was right. We could win the game. I hurried to first base. Once there, I decided I would try to steal second. David knew what I had in mind. He kept a close eye on me.

I went for it on his first pitch. The catcher was slow throwing the ball to second base. I was safe standing up.

Timmy hit a clean line drive a couple of pitches later. I scored easily. The game was over. Nick dashed out of the dugout and lifted me into the air. Timmy pumped my hand. It was great to win. I loved baseball.

My mother invited everyone back to our house. We built a big fire in the backyard and had a weenie roast. The evening was warm but there was plenty of ice-cold lemonade. David came up to me while I was munching on my third hot dog.

"Nice steal," he said.

*I forgot I was mad at him. "Thanks. You were throwing great today."*

*"Couldn't beat you guys, though," he said.*

*"Hey, why don't you pitch for us tomorrow?"*

*He was surprised. "You'd let me?"*

*"Sure. Why not?"*

*"Michael!" my mother called to me from inside the house.*

# Chapter 15

"Michael," Sati said softly. I opened my eyes. She was sitting beside me on the couch, her hand on my head. Quickly, she put her finger to her lips and nodded to Jenny, who was sound asleep and curled up beneath my arm. "Come," Sati whispered, standing.

A minute later, we sat together at the kitchen table. It was dark outside. The wonderful vibes in the air had diminished, although the feeling around Sati was pleasant as always.

"Where's the yogi?" I asked.

"He left a few minutes ago."

"What did you two talk about?"

"The weather."

"Seriously," I said.

"We discussed who would be responsible for making the sun come up next year."

"I see you're in a funny mood."

Her big eyes shone. "I am completely ful-filled."

"Aren't you always?"

"The depth of the ocean never changes. Only the surface waves change. Today I felt the thrill of a tidal wave."

"He seemed like a neat guy," I said. "I hope he didn't think it was rude that I fell asleep."

"It was to be expected."

"You know, I had this wonderful dream," I said. "I was a kid in this small town. It was summer and all we had to do was play baseball and eat all day. Nick, Timmy, and Dave were there. Nothing wild happened, but it was still neat. We played a game of ball and our side won. Then we had hot dogs. I felt sad when you woke me. I grew up here in L.A., but in this town, I felt completely at home."

Sati listened closely. "Are you sure I wasn't there?" she asked.

"I don't think so. Do you like baseball?"

"I prefer to sit in the stands and shout words of encouragement."

"What do you mean?"

"Did you get a hit the first time you were up?"

"No."

"But you hit the ball far," she said.

I felt a strange tingling at the base of my

spine. "That's what my mother told me," I said so softly I could hardly hear the words.

"That was me." She leaned forward, to where her face was only inches from my own. "Now I want you to take me to my home."

My heart was pounding. Her reference had been too accurate be a coincidence. "Can you really see inside my head?"

"I see all of you," she said.

"What did this dream mean?"

"Nothing."

"Please, tell me."

"It was a latent impression of something that hasn't happened yet. It was a premonition, but also a memory. Does that help? I didn't think so. Don't ask me about dreams."

"But you were really there, in that small town?"

"Yes. And tonight, you'll see a portion of my town. Take me home, Michael."

"Where is your home?" I asked.

"In the desert, where you found me. Where I was born."

I swallowed, understanding at last. For a long time now, she had been telling me *she* was my mother, that she was everyone's mother. Now it was clear what she meant when she stepped out of Timmy's hospital room right after he died.

I began to believe, not that she was God, but that she *might* be God. The possibility filled me with such joy, I was terrified.

"Why did these men come today?" I asked.

"To visit me."

"But why today?"

She ignored my question. "I called Linda. She'll be here soon to pick up Jennifer. We can leave before she arrives. Your daughter will be safe."

I held her eyes a long time. "*Who* are you?"

"Sati."

She would tell me no more. We made ready to leave. A few minutes later, going down the apartment stairs with Sati, I heard my phone ring. I was afraid the noise would wake Jenny and that she would want to come. I dashed back to answer it. My fears about my daughter proved groundless; she was out cold. I took the call in the kitchen. Sati had not followed me back up the stairs.

"Hello?"

"Mike, this is Dave. I've got to talk to you. Are you alone?"

"Sort of. Where have you been? A lot has happened. Nick and Mary got married."

David wasn't interested. "I've been searching for Kathy Lion. I've found her."

"*What?*"

David's voice was uneven. "I was going to check into Sati's background, anyway. Then when I saw what she did in the hospital . . . Mike, she was going to *heal* Timmy. She would have done it if he had let her. You saw that, didn't you? She wasn't bluffing."

I nodded, closing my eyes. "I know."

David took a breath. "I drove to Catson yesterday. I talked to Casey Barbers, like you did. I dug up everything I could on Kathy. It seems there was this guy in town she used to see occasionally. I went to his house. I had to slip him a hundred to get in his door. Turned out he'd received a postcard from Kathy a few days before. It had her L.A. address on it."

"It wasn't my address?" I asked.

"It was a place in Hollywood." He paused. "I went there."

My throat was dry. "What does she look like?"

"She's blond and has blue eyes. She's not as pretty as Sati, but she looks a lot like her. But if you think about it, so do a bunch of girls. She works in a topless joint."

"Oh, God."

"Mike, why did you tell me Sati was Kathy based on what Barbers told you? Couldn't you see that slob's as blind as a bat?"

"She wasn't that bad with her glasses on."

"When I was there, she couldn't find her damn glasses!"

"Why are you so angry?" I asked.

"Let me ask you a question? Do you know who you're living with?"

"Sati."

"And who is Sati?"

I felt weak. I leaned against the wall. "I don't know."

We listened to each other's breathing for a minute. In silence David sounded more scared than angry; he was practically panting. "I've got to go," I said finally.

"Where?" he asked.

"I don't know." I wasn't lying.

David paused. "We've got to know, Mike. Soon. You understand?"

Perhaps the three wise men had come to say goodbye to her. "I wonder if we'll be given the chance," I said.

Sati and I rode by Pete's diner at two in the morning. Sati sat silent through most of the drive, sometimes with her eyes closed, other times staring off into the distance, tugging absently on her long hair, her bare feet tucked under her dress. As on the first night, I couldn't quit looking at her.

"Slow," she whispered when we were five miles from Catson.

"Are we going to park?"

"Not yet. We will take the car across the sand."

"Through these tumbleweeds?" I asked. We were in my Honda.

"There's a path. I will show you."

Sati's path wasn't much different from the rest of the desert. The loose gravel scratched the bottom of the chassis, and the bumps gave my shocks a workout they didn't need. Yet I took strange pleasure in simply driving off the side of the road and disappearing into the night. All during the years I had driven my truck, I had felt like a slave to the road. Sati was right, I had to sell my truck.

My windshield wiper water reservoir was

empty. The dust quickly piled up on the glass. Soon I was leaning halfway out the window to see where I was going. We were heading straight north. The lights of Catson faded into a glow on the horizon, and then disappeared altogether. The dry shrubs and cacti, caught in the snapshots of my bouncing headlights, looked like vegetation from another planet. I hoped Sati knew where we were going.

"Stop," she said suddenly.

I hit the brakes. "Are we there?"

"We will walk now."

"We can't drive any farther?"

"There is a ravine less than a hundred yards in front of us." She opened her door. "We will walk."

Being a practical-minded individual, I was worried about little things like dehydration and snakes. It was night, but the temperature was in the low eighties and the air was bone dry. I had once been bitten by a rattlesnake while walking in the desert. It had been no fun. Sati waved away my concerns. She did, however, have me bring a flashlight.

We set off at a respectable clip, the hem of Sati's white dress swishing an inch above the ground. I tried to remember the last time I had changed my flashlight batteries. The night was as black as a buried cavern, the stars as bright as deep space.

I was glad Sati had remembered the ravine. Had we gone into it head first in the car, we wouldn't have gotten out. On foot, though, the barrier was easily crossed. Emerging on the far side, Sati pointed to a shadow slicing across the sky. It was a nearby hill, a steep one at that.

Sati was not in a talkative mood. She wore the wooden sandals she had worn when we met. She moved effortlessly, soundlessly. The dry air irritated my throat. When we reached the hill and began to climb, my legs quickly tired. I began to pant. Sati offered to carry the flashlight. Big deal, I thought, it only weighed a few ounces. I told her it was no problem. I was too much of a man to ask for a break.

The dirt on the hill was different from the dirt on the desert below. It was firmer for one thing. Stooping for a moment to pluck a pebble from my shoe, I also noticed it was rich in quartz particles. They sparkled brightly in the beam of my light. It was easy to imagine we were actually climbing a mountain of diamonds.

Two-thirds of the way to the top, we came to a stream. By this time my thirst was a big ugly monster choking my throat. But when I knelt to drink, Sati stopped me.

"It springs from the summit," she said. "Drink from there."

She knew her home. When we reached the top, I was overjoyed to discover the fountain she had promised. The water bubbled from a crack running between two slabs of hard stone. Burying my face in the cool liquid, I hardly cared that I was drinking from what at the very least was a geological oddity.

Sati wasn't thirsty. She strolled casually

about the flat hilltop. The way she moved and gestured, it was almost as if she were having a conversation with someone unseen. But she spoke no words until she spoke to me.

"Turn off your flashlight, Michael."

"But we might stumble and fall off the edge," I said.

She stepped toward me, her hand outstretched. "Take my hand, I won't let you fall." Her fingers closed around mine, soft and comforting. I turned off the light. The stars shone brighter than before. She added softly, "Only my hand is real."

The Milky Way flowed across the sky. Even before Sati explained, I knew why she had brought me to the spot. As a youngster, I used to go camping in the mountains. In my sleeping bag, before closing my eyes, I would try to count all the stars in the sky. I suppose kids everywhere did. Of course I always dozed off before I could finish. There were too many of them, not an infinite number perhaps, but close enough to make no difference. Infinity was a big word. It was a word Sati often used to describe who she really was. At that moment, standing beside her on the starry hilltop, it was easier to grasp things too big for words. I knew she had brought me there to help me understand her better.

"This is your hometown?" I asked finally, my thoughts lost in the black sky. Her words seemed to come to me from several directions.

"There is a school of thought in this world

that says each planet and constellation in the heavens influences a person's life. It says if you are born at a certain time in a certain place, you will be a certain person. If you are born in another time and place, you will be someone else. No two people are ever born at exactly the same time, in exactly the same place, and for this reason, no two people can ever be exactly alike. This is a belief, and it does not matter whether it is true or not. What does matter is that each planet and each star in the sky shines through me. I am all people, all possibilities. I am a perfect crystal. I am the focus of all the stars in the universe. I am the Starlight Crystal. I am Sati." She paused. "Sit, Michael, and rest. Together we will enjoy the silence of my true nature."

I settled onto the sandy ground. Sati continued to hold on to my hand. Her touch was potent. It was not long before I felt myself sinking deep inside. It was nice, very relaxing. I was pretty sure I didn't go to sleep. It seemed that only minutes passed before she asked me to open my eyes. But by then the sun had already risen into the sky.

# Chapter 16

All who are born, die. Those were Sati's own words. She never said she was an exception to the rule. Sati stared at the glass of orange juice when Mary handed it to her. Later, I was to remember the lesson of the sour milk. But Sati didn't take her own advice; she didn't smell the juice. I suppose it's useless to ask if she knew the drink was poisoned.

It was the evening of the day we had begun in the desert. The whole gang was gathered in my living room: David, Linda, Jenny, Nick, Mary, Mrs. Hutchinson, Fred, and Lori. It had been a long day for me. I had seen the morning sun bright above the desert landscape, and now, sitting in a chair by the west window, I watched as it set into the ocean. The drive home from Arizona had gone quickly. I did not feel tired.

"Is that fresh-squeezed?" I asked as Sati set the juice beside her on a tray. I turned away from the sunset.

"Yes," Mary said. "Would you like some? We've plenty of oranges."

"Don't bother," I said. "My system can't tolerate unprocessed food."

"How come you never talk about diet?" Lori asked Sati. "Isn't it important for our spiritual evolution? Shouldn't we all be vegetarians?"

"If we were all vegetarians, every fast-food joint in the country would go out of business," Fred said with a laugh. "It would ruin the economy."

"But eating meat is like eating a dead animal," Lori protested. She and Fred were arguing constantly these days. It was fun to watch.

"Most meat has dead animals in it," Linda agreed. She had only stopped by my apartment to drop Jenny off. By unspoken agreement, the two of us were maintaining a respectable distance from each other.

"Mary once cooked me a hamburger made from soy beans," Nick said. "It tasted like cardboard."

"I think I burned it," Mary confessed, sitting on the floor beside Nick. They had enjoyed their stay in the mountains, but had returned early to be with Sati. The Goodwill had cleared out the stuff Sati and I had moved into their apartment. The trouble was, they had also taken

Nick and Mary's furniture in the process. Nick said he'd call them tomorrow. He wasn't upset. He was a happily married man.

"During the Depression, my mother used to make us burgers out of beans," Mrs. Hutchinson said nostalgically. "Back then, I thought they tasted just fine."

"What is the Depression?" Jenny asked.

"That's when people were poor after the First World War, dear." Mrs. Hutchinson smiled. "It was a long time ago. I was your age then."

"You weren't old?" Jenny asked, astounded.

"Remember that movie we watched last night on TV with the gangsters?" Linda said to Jenny. "That was the Depression."

"Speaking of TV, are those reporters coming back tonight?" Nick asked David.

"What?" David said.

"The reporters?" Nick repeated. "Are they coming back tonight?"

David was standing slouched between the living room and kitchen. He looked as if he needed a good night's sleep. "I don't know."

"They said they'd be back," Fred remarked. "I bet you knock them dead, Sati."

"You're rude, you know that?" Lori told Fred. "I asked Sati an important question about diet. And before she could answer, you completely changed the subject."

"I did not," Fred said. "It was Mrs. Hutchinson who brought up the Depression. Besides, it was a stupid question, anyway."

Lori fumed, then made an effort to pretend he

didn't exist. "Sati, what advice would you give us as far as our diet is concerned?" she asked politely.

Sati picked up the glass of orange juice. Without hesitating, she drank it down to the last drop. Then she sat staring at the far wall, her face paling, something akin to surprise flickering in the depths of her eyes. "Don't take poison," she whispered.

The gang laughed. But Sati did not laugh. She continued to stare at the wall. She took a couple of deep breaths. The color in her cheeks faded further. I sat up, puzzled.

"I told you it was a stupid question," Fred said to Lori.

"And how do you know what she means by poison?" Lori asked. "I bet she considers meat a poison. Don't you, Sati?"

Sati suddenly clenched her eyes shut and bent forward. Her hair hung over her crossed legs. I leapt to her side and put my hand on her back. "What's wrong?" I asked.

"Poison," she muttered. "In the juice."

I can't take bad news. I just can't. "What are you talking about?" I asked.

Sati sat up slowly, with my help. The skin on her face and arms was as white as a bedsheet. Beneath my fingers, her flesh shook with tiny spasms. She tried to smile. "Oh, Michael," she said.

I picked up her empty glass. I was scared. The few drops of juice that remained smelled like death. "Are you sick?" I asked. "Should I call for an ambulance?"

"You moron!" Fred shouted, jumping up. "She just said she's been poisoned!"

"Mary, what was in that juice?" Nick demanded.

"Oranges," Mary cried.

Linda moved to Sati's side. "If you think you've drunk something bad," she said, "it's vital you vomit it immediately."

"I'll call the hospital," Mrs. Hutchinson said. She picked up the phone with trembling hands, and immediately dropped it to the floor. It was all happening too fast. "Oh, God," she said.

"Yes, you've got to throw up," I said. I grabbed Sati's arm and tried to pull her to her feet. "Come into the bathroom with me. Stick your finger down your throat. It worked wonders for me."

Sati refused to stand. "Let me be. The poison has already entered my system. It's too late."

"No, you've got to get it out of your stomach," I insisted, still trying to get her to stand. Sati gained a measure of control over the pain racking her body and put her hand on mine. She gently undid my fingers from her arm. Her breathing was ragged, as Timmy's had been, but her blue eyes were calm.

"It's time," she said. "I have to go."

"No." I shook my head. "You can't go. You just got here."

Sati looked to the others. They were running around like chickens with their heads missing.

But they froze as her eyes touched each of them. Once again, as in the hospital, they stood waiting for a miracle.

"There is little time," Sati said. "No words can convey what I would have you know. But I will say I want you to remember me. I want you to think of me from time to time. And I want you to be happy. From the beginning of time, this has been my only wish for you." She suppressed a grimace. "Tell all those who came to my meetings that I left for another place. Tell them you don't know the place. That's all. Don't tell them I died. You won't be lying. I never die. I go on and on."

"But you can't leave us," Fred pleaded. "You still have so much to teach us."

Sati shook her head. "I did not come as a teacher. I came to play. And it has been fun. But now, the play is through. Don't feel sad. This body may suffer, but I do not. It's beneath my dignity. Don't feel obligated to tell others about me. Don't become martyrs. But if someone should ask, if they want to know, you may tell them of the days when Sati was here. Tell them . . ." A convulsion shook her body. She had to close her eyes to control it. "Tell them that I am God, that we are all God, and that this can be experienced in silence." Her head slumped on her shoulders. "Now go, all of you, except for Michael, and wait outside. Let's have no tears. It's just a body that leaves you. The Goddess is with you always."

They did as she asked. They filed silently out

of the apartment. Only Jenny came forward. With the others gone, Sati slowly opened her eyes. She could barely support herself upright. She smiled as Jenny laid a white carnation in her lap.

"I don't want you to go," my daughter said, tears falling from her cheeks.

"One carnation, one life," Sati whispered, picking up the flower. "That is enough for anyone to find me. You, Jennifer, will do that. Before you leave this world, you will see me again. I promise you this." Sati hugged her weakly. "Go to your mother, but remember who your real mother is. It is me."

"I know," Jenny whispered. She dried her tears and kissed Sati's cheek. Then she left the apartment, closing the door behind her. The poison was choking off Sati's lungs. She sat with her head down for a couple of minutes, fighting for breath. Finally, she spoke: "I left the recipe for my cookies on top of the icebox."

"Sati," I said, but it was more of a moan.

She pushed herself erect. Her blue eyes peered at me through her tangled hair. "Don't you like my cookies? They could change your life."

My heart was breaking. "Are you really going to die?"

She nodded.

"Who poisoned you?" I asked.

"Does it matter?"

"Tell me."

"I won't. You tell me what you discovered

when you went searching for my true identity."

"I found someone who identified you as a girl named Kathy Lion." I felt ashamed. "I don't know, she said it was you. I wanted to believe you, but I just couldn't. I was afraid I'd be disappointed when the truth came out."

Despite her physical pain, Sati was amused. "You could have found thousands who could have identified me. I reside in all hearts. It shouldn't surprise you that so many should see me and think I look familiar."

I swallowed. "You really are God, aren't you?"

"Yes."

In that moment, there was no place for doubt. I believed her. I was sitting with the supreme being. I had always sat beside her. She was inside me.

"Will you rise on the third day?" I asked.

"No." A fit of coughing shook her. "Bury me on the hill, beneath the stars."

"If that's what you want."

Summoning the last of her strength, she raised her hand and touched my face. And she smiled, one last time. It was such a beautiful smile. It shone with the light of the sun and the moon, and the stars. The Starlight Crystal, she had called herself, and it was true. She was a jewel that only the heavens could have made.

"Before I came," she said, "you thought of Linda constantly. You were miserable. But now you can think of me. You can just think my name, and your life will be filled with joy. You can even write a story about me." She closed her eyes. "There is no poison on these lips. Kiss me goodbye, Michael. I love you."

I kissed her. She kissed me. Then she rested her head on my shoulder and died.

# Chapter 17

There was light in the east when David and I finished digging the grave. Unlike the day before, however, there would be no beautiful sunrise. A murky overcast stretched from horizon to horizon, casting the desert in dismal colors. My back ached. The two of us had carried Sati's body from the car to the top of the hill. That had not been too difficult; unfortunately, the hilltop soil was rock hard. The high quartz content was probably to blame. It had taken us three hours to carve a six-foot hole.

"I've got to rest," David said. He dropped his pick and climbed out of the hole. I followed him, but held on to my shovel. We sat on a boulder not far from the fresh spring beside which Sati lay. She wore her white dress but it wasn't visible; she was wrapped from head to toe in an orange blanket. David gave her a nervous glance.

"She's not getting up," I reassured him.

David sighed and wiped the perspiration from his eyes. He pulled out a cigarette. "I wasn't worried about that."

"What are you worried about?"

He lit his cigarette. "This ground is like concrete. It's killing me."

"The worst is over," I said. "We're down deep enough."

"I don't think so. This is an illegal burial." He puffed on his cigarette. "Let's go another couple of feet."

"What are you worried about?" I repeated.

"Do you have to ask? Hundreds of people met Sati. A lot of them are going to want to know where she went."

"She told us what to say."

He snorted. "Her answer isn't going to satisfy anybody."

"But no one in our group will admit she's dead. They won't disregard her request. And as far as we can tell, she doesn't have a past." I ran my hands along the handle of my shovel. "I just can't understand why you're so worried."

David stared at me. "What's your problem?"

"I needed your help to get her up here and dig the grave. Sure, I could have brought Nick, but then I couldn't have been alone with you. This way . . ." I shrugged. "The grave is ready, and here we are."

He put out his cigarette. "I don't know what you're talking about."

"It's called murder," I said.

He started to stand. I put my hand on his arm. I had only twenty pounds on him; nevertheless, he knew as well as I that I had twice his strength. He sat back down.

"Mike?" he said.

"Why did you do it?"

"Do what? I didn't do anything."

"Why did you poison her?" I asked.

"Did she tell you that?"

"What if she did?"

"Did she?"

"No. She didn't have to."

His eyes strayed to the end of my shovel. He was getting scared. "Why are you accusing me? Mary gave her the orange juice."

"Are you saying Mary poisoned her?"

"No," he said.

"Then who did? If it wasn't you?"

"I don't know. Maybe Fred's chick."

"Lori adored Sati. Why would she kill her?"

He fidgeted and glanced at the body again. "How do you know she didn't poison herself?" he asked.

"That wasn't her style. She radiated life. She gave life to others. She wouldn't have taken her own life. No, the more I think about it, the clearer it becomes that there are only two people in our group capable of murder. You're one of them."

"Then you also consider Nick a suspect?"

"I didn't say that. Nick would have given his life to protect Sati."

"Then who's number two?" he asked.

"Me."

"You?"

"Yes." I pointed to the grave. "Dave, I'm tired and I'm in pain. My patience has run out. If you don't start talking soon, when I leave here, you're going to be lying in that hole with a whole lot of dirt in your face."

David went very still. "You're bluffing."

"The preacher at the meeting was bluffing. He was a Christian. Do you know when I last went to church? It was ages ago." I tightened my grip on the shovel. "Why did you do it?"

He saw I was serious. He lowered his head. "When I first met Sati, I told you I thought she was great. I'd never seen anyone who could affect people the way she could. You knew I was hoping she'd be famous, that I'd be a part of her fame. I had plans for her. Your story about Kathy Lion wasn't going to slow them down." His voice wavered. "I thought the world of her."

"But you didn't think she was God?" I asked.

He looked at me, angry as well as frightened. "Did you?"

"No. But I didn't kill her."

"Dammit, Mike! She said she could drink poison."

"What? She never said that." I caught myself.

I remembered her remark in the kitchen, when the sour milk had made me sick. "You've got it wrong. She said, 'My tummy works better than yours. I can *almost* drink poison.'"

"That's not what Timmy told me."

I nodded. I also recalled the gathering we'd had after Sati's second meeting. Timmy had accidentally misquoted her, and neither Nick nor I had corrected him.

Sati had once said, while responding to a question regarding the many contradictions in the Bible, that Christ's words had been twisted inside out the same day he had spoken them, even by those closest and dearest to him. It was easy to see how.

"You used the poison to test her?" I asked, appalled. "You had some nerve."

"You wanted to know the truth as badly as I did."

"That's B.S. Didn't you stop to ask yourself, what if her body is no different from ours? What if she dies?"

He nodded weakly. "Yes."

"And?"

He didn't answer my question, not directly. Instead, he began to cry. I almost belted him with the shovel right then and there. Here he murders the greatest person in the world and then he thinks he can cry about it and I'll feel sorry for him.

"I tried to tell you when I got back from Kathy Lion's place," he said finally. "You wouldn't listen to me. I even brought up what she said to

Timmy in the hospital. We both knew she was
serious. *She* knew she could heal him. You said
it yourself."

"So?"

He was a pathetic sight. "I was scared, Mike."

"Of what?"

He closed his eyes and took a deep shudder-
ing breath. "I've done all right with my life. I've
done better than most. Anyone could tell you
that. I've got money. I've got girls. If I didn't
work another day in my life, I could still buy
whatever I wanted." He paused. "Up until she
came along, I had everything."

"I don't recall her ever picking your pockets,"
I said.

"She made everything I owned useless!" His
words dropped to a whisper. "She made my life
useless."

He had poisoned her to make sure she was
God. He had poisoned her to make sure she
wasn't. He was a screwed-up man. Yet I understood him. Sati had never spoken a word about
the evils of materialism. Indeed, she had seemed
to think that money was something to be enjoyed, as much as anything else in the world
was to be enjoyed. Money itself was not at the
crux of David's fear. His problem was the same
one we all shared, to one degree or another. Sati
had turned everything we thought and believed
upside down. But she had not given us a specific system of belief to replace what she had
taken away. She had given us a taste of our
inner silence instead, a taste of ourselves. And

apparently what David had tasted when he had delved deep inside had not been to his liking. No, that is not true. What he had seen when he came back out had not been to his liking. It was very simple. After all, he was a jerk.

"Where did you get the poison?" I asked.

"I sometimes buy cocaine from a guy in Venice," he mumbled. "He got it for me. I think it was cyanide, but I'm not sure."

"Did you pour it in the juice when Mary wasn't looking?"

He nodded, his head hung low. "Please don't kill me, Mike."

I'd lied to him. I'd just wanted to hear the truth. I couldn't kill him, not now, even though I might have done so a few days earlier. My dream of summer baseball games was on my mind. My mother had told me to invite David to be on my team. Of course I had protested at first, but later I'd felt good about asking him to pitch for us. I'd awakened feeling good about it.

I wondered if the yogi had been trying to tell me something.

On the other hand, the symbolic nature of dreams had never mattered to me. Even Sati had minimized their importance. I was probably just looking for an excuse not to brain him.

"I won't kill you," I said finally. "But the desert might."

He looked up. "What do you mean?"

"I'm not giving you a ride back."

"But the sun's coming up. I don't have a canteen. It's twenty miles to the road."

"Then you better get going."

"But—"

"Get out of here," I interrupted, standing. "Now."

A look at my face—and my shovel—convinced him. I followed him with my eyes until he was off the hill, just to be sure he wasn't heading toward my car. But the fear of God was on him. He made straight for the road.

Now came the hard part.

I didn't want to put her in a hole in the ground. She'd repeatedly emphasized that she was more than the body, that the cosmos itself was her actual form, but the charm I'd found in her blue eyes and rich smile was not easily forgotten. My heart was heavy as I placed her body beside the grave and jumped down into the hole. Without David, what I did next should have taxed my strength to the limit. The ground was slightly above my head. As a result, my upstretched arms had to work at an angle of horrible leverage. Yet by some strange magic, she slipped into my hands as if she were but a feather. Her muscle tone was normal. Her limbs had lost no flexibility. That was a minor miracle in itself. She should have been in the throes of rigor mortis. Then again, I reminded myself, some bodies took longer to stiffen up.

I laid her on the floor of the grave and knelt beside her. I pulled the blanket from her face. Was she dreaming of the playtimes of her children, I wondered? Dreaming of all of us who still walked in this world? Looking at her, it

was easy to believe she was only sleeping. But I
didn't pray for her to awaken. She had asked
me to pray only for the ill, not the dead.

"Sati," I said. I picked up her left hand and
slipped the ring Linda had returned to me onto
her ring finger. It fit perfectly. "I love you, too."

I clipped a lock of her hair with my pocket
knife. Wherever she was, I knew she wouldn't
mind.

Filling in the hole took forever.

On the road home, I saw a girl hitchhiking.
She held a cardboard sign that said: L.A.
PLEASE!

I picked her up, what the hell. Her name was
Susan and she had brown hair and green eyes.
She wanted to be an actress.

I didn't take her back to my apartment.

# *Epilogue*

**T**wo years have come and gone since
Sati was here. Everybody in the
inner circle has seen major changes
in that time.

A couple of months after all the excitement,
Fred lost his paper route. He was delivering the
Sunday edition, and this time he didn't hit a
poodle. He hit a police car. It wouldn't have
been so bad had he hit it with a paper instead of
his station wagon. The cop was in a bad mood,
and Fred lost his cool. Lori and I had to bail
him out.

But Lori has stuck with Fred. It would be nice
to say they are fighting less and loving more.
Such is not the case. However, they do appear
to enjoy their fights more. Nowadays, they both

Christopher Pike

work for me. Fred is in charge of deliveries. Lori is my personal secretary.

Mrs. Hutchinson's arthritis never returned. Indeed, the way she goes on, she looks good for another seventy years. She continues to read her Bible every day, and she still attends church. She also works as my company controller. She watches the money. There is plenty of it.

After Sati left, Nick continued to get one fireplace after another. He was never without work. He saved up a tidy sum of money. Then he decided to have plastic surgery on his scar. The cut had been more of an emotional handicap than a physical one. Even though it hampered his getting jobs, he admitted, he had hung onto it because it was his last tie to his mean street days. Surprisingly, when the operation was over and he was looking pretty, his contracting business fizzled. He had no choice. He had to come to work for me. I made him vice-president.

Mary gave birth to a beautiful girl. They named her Tammy, in honor of Timmy. She is so cute, sometimes when I'm playing with her I wonder if anyone will ever want to say boo to her. I know she's going to break a lot of hearts.

Linda married Dick. She also obtained her counseling certificate, but had to give up her practice shortly afterward to take care of a new son. The return to changing diapers does not seem to bother her. For her part, Jenny enjoys having a baby brother, even if he does resemble Dick, whom she continues to despise. Jenny

260

lives with me more often than not. She's in second grade and she's writing a book about Sati.

David barely made it out of the desert. A weekend pilot out for an afternoon cruise spotted him lying face down in the sand not one mile from the highway. The authorities were notified, and an ambulance was sent out. David spent several days in the hospital, suffering from dehydration and a sunburn that practically peeled his face off. I never told anybody about what happened on the hill, but it didn't take the rest of the gang long to figure out why I stranded him. To their credit, and out of respect for Sati's wish, none of them said a word to him. They didn't have to. He knew they knew. When David returned from his stay in the hospital, he began to suffer from what Nick called the Judas syndrome.

David didn't hang himself. He did the next worst thing—he started smoking crack. Mrs. Hutchinson was the only one of us who continued to stay in contact with him. He dropped to 120 pounds, she said, and was beginning to have heart palpitations, when she finally convinced him to check into a detox clinic. Months later, he reemerged, off drugs and married to the doctor who had cured him. He sold his apartments and bought a farm in Nebraska. Word has it that he coaches a Little League team when he's not sowing his fields. I'm happy for him, I really am.

The thought of one day being forced to move

from the apartment where Sati had spent some of her short life bothered me. So I bought the apartments. By the time David was selling the complex, I could afford it.

But I get ahead of myself.

The direction of my life was unclear when Sati died. However, one thing I knew for certain: I had to get out of the trucking business. If the purpose of life was to be happy, I reasoned, and I continued to spend my days doing something that made me miserable, then my life had no purpose at all. I returned the loan David had helped me obtain and put my trucks up for sale. Jesse, my partner, took one off my hands. I sold the other almost immediately. I ended up with ninety grand in my pocket. Linda's lawyer wanted half of it. I gave it to him, and he gave half of it to Linda. He kept the rest for his troubles. She should have just asked me for the money, I thought. Before starting on anything new, I decided to sleep twelve hours a night for a few months, and to rent all the movies I had been meaning to see for the last few years.

The life of a bum suited me well. I got rid of the bags under my eyes and my digestion improved. I even took up surfing again. I got a great tan. It was while I was surfing that I ran into Reverend Green.

"Ran into" can be taken literally here. Three months after Sati's departure, toward the end of summer, a strong south swell hit the L.A. beaches. It was near sundown, and I had been in the water since noon. I was on my last ride. I cut left inside the curl of a wave that was large enough to swallow me whole. Suddenly, the point of a board and a pair of strong legs came down over the top right in front of me. I couldn't see the upper torso. It didn't matter. I knew I was about to be impaled if I didn't make a radical change in direction. Dropping to my knees, I pulled my board into the face of the wave. I wiped out. The saltwater roller coaster lasted for thirty seconds, a long time when I couldn't look at my watch and I didn't have any oxygen in my lungs. When I was finally able to come up for a breath, the fellow who had cut me off paddled over to apologize.

"Sorry," he said. "I didn't see you until I was committed."

I tried to tell him not to worry about it, but I ended up coughing instead. We were in shallow water. He got off his board and offered me a hand. I let him pull me out of the backwash of foam. I continued to choke on what felt like a ten-foot strand of seaweed stuck in my lungs. I hardly looked at him. I was surprised when he said my name.

"Why, Mr. Winters, it's you."

I raised my head. It took me a moment to place him. He didn't have on his suit and tie. And his face had changed. At Sati's meeting, even when he smiled, he had looked frustrated. Now his expression, though startled, was pleasant.

"Reverend Green?" I asked.

He laughed. "Yeah, it's me. What a coincidence we should meet like this. I was just talking to Mrs. Hutchinson this morning for the first time in ages. She brought up your name. I was thinking of stopping by and seeing you." He added, in a softer voice, "I wanted to apologize to you."

I waved my hand. I'd finally got the saltwater out of my chest. "It was nothing, a misunderstanding. Forget it."

"That's kind of you." He glanced out to sea, at the next eight-foot set lining up. "Been out here a while?"

"All day."

"Great, isn't it?"

"Yeah," I said.

"Haven't seen waves like this in years."

"They don't make them like they used to."

He picked up his board. "But it'll be dark soon. I was planning on getting a bite on the pier. Their fish and chips are the best on the West Coast. I'd love it if you could join me."

I was curious about his quitting as minister at Mrs. Hutchinson's church. "Sounds good," I said.

We stashed our boards in his car and walked the mile to the pier. He talked enthusiastically about a home for runaway kids he had opened in Hollywood. He was currently taking care of forty youngsters. Apparently, he'd recently received a huge anonymous donation that had allowed him to start the home. The money had arrived through the mail with no instructions as to how it was to be spent.

He was no longer associated with a particular church.

It was only when we were eating our greasy food, sitting on a bench overlooking the water, the swells smooth and purple in the fading light, that the conversation turned to me. By this time I'd begun to feel comfortable with him. The nastiness of our original meeting was indeed forgotten. I spoke to him as if he was *my* minister. I told him of my indecision over my future career. He listened attentively.

"If I had the money," I said in closing, "I think I'd spend the rest of my life surfing."

He smiled. "I know the feeling. Lately, I've been trying to get down here at least once a week."

"It must be tough with all those kids hanging on to you."

"I make the time." He paused, thinking. "Did she ever give you any direction?"

He wanted to talk about her, I could tell. "Sati seldom gave specific advice. She didn't like to infringe on people's free will."

He nodded, watching the seagulls. "Mrs. Hutchinson tells me she's gone away."

"Yes," I said.

"Do you ever hear from her?"

"I'm afraid not."

"Do you think she'll be coming back?"

"You'd like to see her again, wouldn't you?"

"Yes. I should have gone to her meetings when I had the chance. Mrs. Hutchinson gave me the impression she has left the area for good."

"I think so."

He spoke wistfully. "She was a beautiful woman."

I can be blunt at times. "Do you think she was God?"

"Yes."

I ate a french fry. "That's amazing."

He sighed and rested his feet on the pier railing. "When I left the meeting that night, I was confused. I didn't know why. She was the last person who should've upset me. She wasn't saved. She obviously knew nothing about the Bible. Worst of all, I told myself, she was a blasphemer. People like her were sure to go to hell." He shrugged. "I wanted to chalk her off as a lost cause and forget about her."

"Why couldn't you?"

"It could have been several things. Maybe it was the look she gave me when I threatened her with the hammer and nail. Her eyes were soft, loving. She wasn't scared at all. She wasn't mad at me. It was as if she understood what I was doing, and why. And she forgave me. When I got back to my place, I asked myself again and again how someone with such love could be the devil's agent. I got down on my knees and prayed for an answer. Always before, whenever I prayed to God, he always gave me an answer. Or at least I thought he did."

"And this time?"

Mr. Green put his food down. "At the beginning of her meeting, she told us to sit quietly. Naturally, I kept my eyes open the entire time so I'd be safe from any negative influence. Then later, when she referred to the silent side of her nature, I didn't know what she was talking about. I'd felt nothing. But when I was alone in my room and praying for guidance, something happened. My body did not stop in the way she talked about, but it went still. Then my mind got quiet. I had my eyes open, I was conscious and everything, but I suddenly felt as if I were slipping into a wonderful dreamland where everything was perfect. No, I shouldn't say that. Everything looked the same. My carpet still needed cleaning. My walls needed scrubbing. Nothing had really changed. It was just that I no longer cared that everything wasn't perfect, and because I didn't care, it *was* perfect. Does that make sense?"

I remembered the time I had sat with Sati right after Timmy had met her, how delightful the sun had felt on my arm, how the very air had seemed to reverberate with contentment. "Yes," I said.

He nodded. "I hesitate to call it a religious experience. I didn't see God. Nothing was revealed to me. But the peace I felt then was unbelievable. I would eat something, I would walk around the block, and it would be so much fun. Even now, I still feel it. And I know who gave it to me." He looked at me and put his hand on my arm. "It was her. It was Sati."

"But you were praying to God when all this started," I said.

"It was she who gave it to me, Mike. I can't explain it. I knew it was Sati then and I know it now."

"And this is why you think she was God?"

"Yes," he said.

"Then why didn't you go to more of her meetings?"

He sighed again. "Something kept me away. Perhaps it was her will."

"She told me the night you challenged her that you wouldn't return to her meetings."

The comment did not depress him as I feared it might. He actually smiled. "She talked about me?" he asked.

"She compared the two of us. She said we were both obsessed with images that had nothing to do with reality. Your image was of Jesus. Mine was of my ex-wife."

He nodded. "In my mind, the Lord was always bleeding over the sorrows of the world. But when I experienced such wonder that night, I knew that was impossible. God couldn't suffer. I didn't have to suffer." He let go of my arm and sat back on the bench. "She's left her body, hasn't she?"

I averted my eyes. "I don't know where she's gone."

"That's OK, Mike. I understand."

We sat for a while in silence, the waves breaking beneath our feet. Suddenly, he chuckled.

"What is it?" I asked.

"I remember how she offered me one of her cookies, how I turned it down. I sure wish I had that cookie now."

"I could make you some. She left me the recipe."

"Is that so? I must get it from you. How do they taste?"

"Sweet. I like them. Everyone seems to." It was my turn to chuckle. "Before she left, Sati said those cookies could change my life."

Mr. Green sat up. "Really? What do you think she meant by that?"

"Nothing. Sati was always joking around."

"But maybe she was trying to tell you something."

"I don't think so."

"But you say everyone likes them?" he asked.

"Yeah."

"Does *anyone* dislike them?"

"I've never seen anyone turn them down, if that's what you mean."

Mr. Green got excited. "Mike, do you realize what you're saying? Sati's left you with a product no one can resist."

"Huh?"

"You just told me how you can't stand the thought of going back to being a truck driver. As far as I can see, you have a perfect way out. Go into the cookie business!"

"But the only cookie I know how to make is hers. I can't open a bakery and only sell one product."

"Why not? As long as it's a great product, it doesn't matter. Look, I'm serious about this. I'm going to help finance you."

"No way. You need your money for your kids. I'd be taking the food out of their mouths."

"I said I'd help you. I won't give you my last penny. You'll have to put up the dough you got for your trucks."

"But my ex-wife wants some more of that."

"Do you *have* to give it to her?"

"No, but . . ."

He laughed. He was having a great time. "But what? Do you want her lawyer to make any more off you?"

The light was beginning to dawn. "What would I need to get started?" I asked.

Mr. Green explained it to me. All we needed was money. He was adamant that I give Sati's recipe the best possible chance, right from the start. He wanted to open a shop in the heart of Beverly Hills. I said fine. The next day we checked with real estate people. We met with instant luck. A croissant joint in a choice location had gone under the previous week. The owner was looking for someone to take over his lease for the next six months, at half the going rate. Mr. Green took it as a favorable omen. We rented the place.

We had a shop, now we needed a name and a way to produce the cookies in respectable numbers. We tossed around all sorts of titles: Divine Delights, Cosmic Cookies, Sati's Satori—it was

L.A. after all. In the end, I decided simplicity would serve us best. I called the shop The Cookie. I hoped the public would see our cookies as the final word on the subject.

I did not know there were actually machines you could buy that put the top and bottom halves of cookies together. I soon found out, and we spent another sizable portion of our resources obtaining one. But it was worth it. Give that thing the tiny shortbread circles and gallons of jam and it would do the rest.

The secret ingredient in Sati's recipe was a combination of flavors, herbs, and spices that were mixed directly into the shortbread dough. In all the times she had made the cookies with the others, she had never revealed their exact formula. The amount of "elixir" present in each cookie was relatively small. I decided I would personally handle that portion of the baking process. Why not, I thought? If she had wanted everyone to know the secret, she would have told me to mail it to a women's magazine.

Fred and Lori helped out. Fred's attitude toward food in relationship to evolution had undergone a complete turnaround. He had dispensed with normal diets. He was into fasting. Helping me set up the cookie shop, he ate nothing but The Cookie for a week. His acne got much worse.

For any new business, advertisement is essential. Here we broke completely from tradition. After her initial flyers, Sati had depended solely on word of mouth to announce her meetings. We decided to follow a similar course. We printed up five thousand sheets extolling The Cookie. Then we mailed them into the surrounding neighborhoods and sat back and waited.

Opening day finally arrived. At first business was pitifully slow. On day one we sold a grand total of 108 cookies. At fifty cents apiece, I couldn't even expect to be able to pay the rent. On day two, we sold 316 cookies. But this figure had been artificially inflated. Lori had called up a dozen friends and talked them into coming down. The whole first week was a disaster. Fred and Mr. Green looked upon it as a test of faith.

Then things took off like a rocket. Business went from zero to sixty overnight. People started to pour in. It was the same for everybody—they had heard about us from a friend, or from a friend of a friend. They did not want *a* cookie, they wanted *dozens* of cookies. And when they returned, they brought *dozens* of friends. The question they asked was always the same: "What do you put in these? They're fantastic!"

Mr. Green continued to offer his support, but with his home for kids, he was seldom able to come by the store. Nevertheless, when he learned of our uncanny success, he wanted us to expand. By the third month, I was already in the black, and I was a believer. I took out a loan—from the same bank and the same loan officer who had initially refused the loan for my truck—and opened a second store by the beach where

Sati used to walk. I put Nick in charge of it, and the store did as well as the first. We could not make the cookies fast enough.

This entrepreneurial tale could go on and on. But this is Sati's story. Suffice it to say I have opened up two more stores in the area and the whole gang is now working for me. Our success has been in the news. Local businessmen approach me every other day to sell franchises, and go nationwide. I thought about it for a while, but I decided I like having the business small and familylike. We have enough money. It's given me plenty of free time, which is the only reason I wanted money in the first place. I figure if I open more stores, I'll have to start doing real work again.

I feel pretty good these days. I know many will scoff at this, but I honestly don't think it's the money that has made the big difference in my life. I should explain.

A year after Sati left, Nick and I were driving across the city on a business trip. We were talking volume and dollars when we suddenly fell silent and stared at each other for several seconds. Then we began to laugh our heads off.

"It's still there, isn't it?" he asked when we finally calmed down.

"It's getting stronger," I replied.

I said at the beginning that Sati did not teach anything. I said this because she herself insisted she was not a teacher. Nevertheless, I do feel she left us with a valuable lesson. She left us with a portion of herself.

In the car, Nick and I were talking about the experience of inner silence. Because it's not the experience of something specific, not even a feeling in the usual sense of the word, it's difficult to talk about. But it's definitely real. At times, it seems more real than anything in the external world.

And it makes the external world far more enjoyable. It used to be that when I saw people on TV discussing how they found inner peace, I would get annoyed. Perhaps I was jealous, I don't know. But I always felt that whatever they were saying should be kept private. Now I'm just like them. Not that I go around lecturing and preaching. I remember Sati's advice about becoming a martyr. But when I'm at the store getting groceries, and the clerk asks me how I'm doing, I smile and say "Great." I know I used to do that, but at least now I mean it.

I want to be serious, but it's hard. I'm like the little kid who plays outside all day and has all the fun in the world, but only because he knows his mother is at home waiting for him. That's what it's like to be still inside. Mother is at home. Everything will eventually work out. Everything is inevitable. She is *always* at home. My thoughts do not support my inner silence; it is just there. It doesn't even go away when I sleep. I doubt it will when I die.

By no means does this mean I have arrived at the state that Sati described as enlightenment. As before, I have my ups and downs. But I would also have to say that more and more I find myself *watching* my joys and sorrows. They are there, they are real; they just don't affect me as they did before. Now, the average person might call this the growth of apathy, or worse, schizophrenia. All I can say is that I have never felt more sensitive or sane. My friends have noticed the same thing in their own lives. Even Fred.

Sati's prediction has come true—I no longer dwell on Linda. I contemplate my blue-eyed friend instead. She made me happy when she was here. She makes me happy now. I miss her, true, but I also feel she is not far away.

Occasionally I run into someone who attended her meetings. A few ask what became of her. Most appear content to remember her in the company of someone else who had met her. The word is spreading around town, on the wind perhaps, about who was here. I wouldn't be surprised if years from now her name is known in every corner of the globe.

Was Sati God? When she was here, that question was important to me. I still don't know the answer to it. And now, I don't care to know.

She was wonderful. She had grace and beauty, love and power. Nothing could hurt her or drag her down. The insults thrown at her from strangers, the doubts dumped on her from friends—they flowed off her like water poured over the back of a swan. Her compassion for those who suffered was outweighed only by her complete unattachment to them. Some might say she was indifferent. I know now her ocean of joy was simply too vast to be disturbed by any wave. Even her own death made her laugh.

Mother Sati.

If she wasn't God, she was everything God should be.

# THE DRAGON REBORN

**Sequel to The Great Hunt**

**Book Three**
~of~
**The Wheel of Time**

by

## Robert Jordan

### Praise for *Eye of the World*

"A powerful vision of good and evil...fascinating people moving through a rich and interesting world."  —Orson Scott Card

"Richly detailed...fully realized, complex adventure."
—*Library Journal*

"A combination of Robin Hood and Stephen King that is hard to resist...Jordan makes the reader care about these characters as though they were old friends."  —*Milwaukee Sentinel*

### Praise for *The Great Hunt*

"Jordan can spin as rich a world and as event-filled a tale as [Tolkien]...will not be easy to put down."  —*ALA Booklist*

"Worth re-reading a time or two."  —*Locus*

"This is good stuff...Splendidly characterized and cleverly plotted...The Great Hunt is a good book which will always be a good book. I shall certainly [line up] for the third volume."
—*Interzone*

# The Dragon Reborn
*coming in hardcover in August, 1991*

# BESTSELLERS
# FROM TOR

| | | | |
|---|---|---|---|
| ☐ ☐ | 50570-0 | ALL ABOUT WOMEN<br>Andrew M. Greeley | $4.95<br>Canada $5.95 |
| ☐ ☐ | 58341-8<br>58342-6 | ANGEL FIRE<br>Andrew M. Greeley | $4.95<br>Canada $5.95 |
| ☐ ☐ | 52725-9<br>52726-7 | BLACK WIND<br>F. Paul Wilson | $4.95<br>Canada $5.95 |
| ☐ ☐ | 51392-4 | LONG RIDE HOME<br>W. Michael Gear | $4.95<br>Canada $5.95 |
| ☐ ☐ | 50350-3 | OKTOBER<br>Stephen Gallagher | $4.95<br>Canada $5.95 |
| ☐ ☐ | 50857-2 | THE RANSOM OF BLACK STEALTH One<br>Dean Ing | $5.95<br>Canada $6.95 |
| ☐ ☐ | 50088-1 | SAND IN THE WIND<br>Kathleen O'Neal Gear | $4.50<br>Canada $5.50 |
| ☐ ☐ | 51878-0 | SANDMAN<br>Linda Crockett | $4.95<br>Canada $5.95 |
| ☐ ☐ | 50214-0<br>50215-9 | THE SCHOLARS OF NIGHT<br>John M. Ford | $4.95<br>Canada $5.95 |
| ☐ ☐ | 51826-8 | TENDER PREY<br>Julia Grice | $4.95<br>Canada $5.95 |
| ☐ ☐ | 52188-4 | TIME AND CHANCE<br>Alan Brennert | $4.95<br>Canada $5.95 |

Buy them at your local bookstore or use this handy coupon:
Clip and mail this page with your order.

Publishers Book and Audio Mailing Service
P.O. Box 120159, Staten Island, NY 10312-0004

Please send me the book(s) I have checked above. I am enclosing $ _____
(please add $1.25 for the first book, and $.25 for each additional book to cover postage and handling.
Send check or money order only—no CODs).

Name _____
Address _____
City _____ State/Zip _____
Please allow six weeks for delivery. Prices subject to change without notice.

# FANTASY BESTSELLERS
# FROM TOR

| | | | |
|---|---|---|---|
| ☐ ☐ | 55852-9 55853-7 | ARIOSTO *Chelsea Quinn Yarbro* | $3.95 Canada $4.95 |
| ☐ ☐ | 53671-1 53672-X | THE DOOR INTO FIRE *Diane Duane* | $2.95 Canada $3.50 |
| ☐ ☐ | 53673-8 53674-6 | THE DOOR INTO SHADOW *Diane Duane* | $2.95 Canada $3.50 |
| ☐ ☐ | 55750-6 55751-4 | ECHOES OF VALOR *edited by Karl Edward Wagner* | $2.95 Canada $3.95 |
| ☐ ☐ | 51181-6 | THE EYE OF THE WORLD *Robert Jordan* | $5.95 Canada $6.95 |
| ☐ ☐ | 53388-7 53389-5 | THE HIDDEN TEMPLE *Catherine Cooke* | $3.95 Canada $4.95 |
| ☐ ☐ | 55446-9 55447-7 | MOONSINGER'S FRIENDS *edited by Susan Shwartz* | $3.50 Canada $4.50 |
| ☐ ☐ | 55515-5 55516-3 | THE SHATTERED HORSE *S.P. Somtow* | $3.95 Canada $4.95 |
| ☐ ☐ | 50249-3 50250-7 | SISTER LIGHT, SISTER DARK *Jane Yolen* | $3.95 Canada $4.95 |
| ☐ ☐ | 54348-3 54349-1 | SWORDSPOINT *Ellen Kushner* | $3.95 Canada $4.95 |
| ☐ ☐ | 53293-7 53294-5 | THE VAMPIRE TAPESTRY *Suzie McKee Charnas* | $2.95 Canada $3.95 |

# MORE BESTSELLING
# FANTASY FROM TOR